The Bexford North/Annie Watson Mystery series
comprise six books, each complete in itself:

1. *And The Dance Goes On*

2. *The Black Lamb*

3. *The Blight of Lady Emily*

4. *The Bell Tolled Twice*

5. *Death and the Lazy Milkmaid*

6. *Death and the Dowagers*

THE BLIGHT OF LADY EMILY

MURDER & MALICE. SYDNEY. WINTER 1943

TONY BRENNAN

ISBN: 978-1-925681-04-8

Published by Vivid Publishing
P.O. Box 948, Fremantle
Western Australia 6959
www.vividpublishing.com.au

Cataloguing-in-Publication data is available from the National Library of Australia

DEDICATION

Once again my thanks to Dr G for helpful medical discussions which I am sure I get all wrong; to my greatest supporter and chief critic, Dr PSB, without whom I would never write anything; and, especially, to all the good, very dear, elderly people who have shared their memories with me of the fearful days of 1942-43 when Australia was suffering so greatly in World War 2.

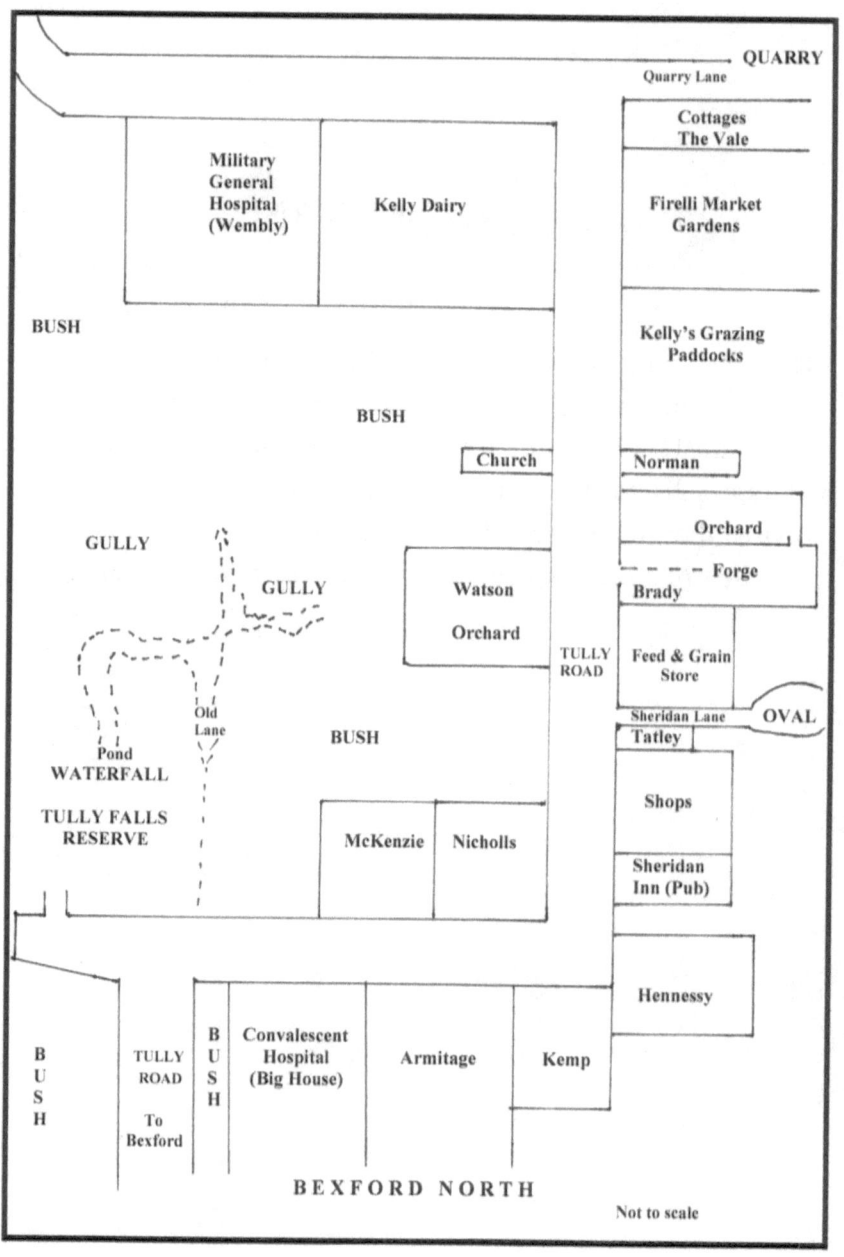

CHAPTER 1

Telephone call to Annie Watson from her aunt, Mother Benedicta. "No, no, no, no. *NO*! … I'm sorry Aunt Benedicta, I can't do it!

"And, why ever not, may I ask?"

"You know damn well, Aunt, what she's like! No… I won't apologize. She's a disaster wherever she goes."

"The poor woman assured me she only wants a little peace and quiet…."

"Are you kidding? She has some nefarious scheme in mind, let me tell you…"

"I've never known you to be so uncharitable, Annie."

"When we're talking about the precious Lady Emily Gascoigne-Ridley, Aunt, charity goes out the window. No, it's no use talking, I can't and I won't, promise to be nice to her, if she comes here to live."

"It's only for the winter, Annie; she's not going to live with you. She's staying at the local Inn."

"God help them: I must warn them about her…"

There was a moment silence on the phone. Both parties were regrouping their arguments. This was broken by the elderly voice of the nun.

"Tell me, Annie," Mother Benedicta asked, "how is Billy?"

"*How is Billy?* …That's a sudden shift in the conversation, isn't it? *What are you up to?* As a matter of fact, my poor lad's been well now for some months; no cardiac attacks, thank heavens." Annie's voice changed; she sounded happy and proud. She rattled on.

"He's doing very well. Ernest Gascoigne-Ridley has provided a brilliant, wounded soldier as a tutor for Billy. He's going to prepare him for the matriculation University exam …"

"Yes I did hear that Ernest had been sponsoring Billy's education…."

The light dawned on poor Annie.

"Ah! Huh! Huh! …So that's it, you devious woman! *Now, I see what you're up to!* Yes, I *am* well aware, that Ernest is the *nephew* of the Lady Emily Gascoigne-Ridley! … All right, all right, *all right!* I admit I have an obligation. Tell me, you tricky schemer, what do you want me to do? Tell me all about it."

As Annie Watson listened as her aunt explained that Lady Emily would be staying *for the entire winter*, she was appalled.

"For the entire winter? She'll go crazy – I mean, more than she is already…"

"Why do you think that, Annie?"

"You know this place; there's absolutely nothing to do here, or see …"

"Oh, no she won't, Annie, she'll be very busy", Benedicta calmly announced. "You see, she recently converted to Communism – she is now dedicated to the cause of world revolution – to rid the world of capitalism and to bring about the triumph of the proletariat.

"She told me it was now her mission in life to use her great wealth for this cause. She would begin the revolution in the little village of Bexford North."

"Now! That proves it! I told you she was off her rocker! Communism in *this* village? She could be lynched; but then, that might solve the family's problem, wouldn't it?"

"Annie!"

"All right I apologize. Of course I don't want the demented woman dead: I just want her anywhere but here."

The elderly voice changed. "I'm really sorry, Annie, but she's determined. I tried to get her to change her mind, but I can't stop her. *She's arriving tomorrow*; I thought I'd better warn you."

"*Tomorrow*! Dear God! Oh well … as it's a fait accompli, we can only pray that the winter may be a severe one!"

"Why is that Annie?"

"Why? Well, she could become so frozen and frost-bittten, she'll have to stay in her room all the time – they have no heating in the pub ... All right, all right, *all right!* I'll go along to the pub, and see she's settled in, *but that's all! …*"

"Perhaps, Annie, you could try to wean her away from her frightening agenda…"

"What? …Don't kid yourself Aunty. You know she hates me, and laughs at me – thinks I'm a nut case …Oh *really*? Well, let me tell you, if I am, I'm in good company *in this family*! You once said I resembled you! Good Morning, Mother Benedicta; I may ring you again and I may not!"

Annie put down the phone and stared angrily at the instrument, as if it were the cause of her woes. In an abstracted manner, she pinned up a large clump of her unwieldy hair which had tumbled down over one eye.

Sighing, suddenly aware how cold it was, she went out to her kitchen, grateful for its warmth. She decided she needed a large cup of tea – her universal panacea for all bad news. She sat down at her table, drinking tea, wondering how on earth she was going to manage this troublesome relation.

The whole winter! There would be more than the freezing weather to cope with now. Well, one thing she must do now; she must go and warn the Joneses at the pub; they had no idea what kind of guest was descending upon them.

The back door of the kitchen slammed open; Annie's son, Billy, came through carrying an armful of books and papers. He was a very tall youngster of fifteen, very thin, with his mother's large blue eyes and the same shock of brown hair. Seeing his mother at the table, Billy dropped the books and greeted her happily.

"You'll never guess what, Mum," he began with his usual enthusiasm, "Dr. Scott gave me an A for my Latin, but only a B+ for the Greek. Guess that means more slogging at the Greek, doesn't it?"

Annie Watson smiled at her tall son, already taller than everyone in the family. "It certainly does, Billy. I wish I could help you, but I've got no Greek at all. The Latin's not so bad, but Greek…

"Doesn't matter, Mum," the boy responded, "Dr Scott is always praising the way you taught me the modern languages; he said it was tremendous, so that's pretty good isn't it?"

"These blasted exams, Billy! Why do they have to include Latin and Greek, anyhow? I know you want to study Classics, but you'd think all the other subjects would be enough – just to get *into* the damn place!

"However," Annie ran her fingers through her hair, "if that's what you want, then please God, and with the help of Cousin Ernest, you'll get there." Annie turned and looked seriously at her son.

"Billy, sit down. I've got something to tell you. A relative of ours is coming to stay in the village – at the pub.

"Oh, do I know them?"

"No, you've never met this woman. She a cousin, actually, another niece of Mother Benedicta."

Billy smiled happily. "Well, if she's anything like Mother Benedicta, she'll be great fun. Aunt Benedicta's a very, very funny, clever lady."

"She is that," conceded his mother, sighing. "Unfortunately, this one is entirely different. I don't know how to say this exactly, Billy, but I don't like her, or even *trust* her."

Billy stared at his mother; this was a very strange thing for her to say about anyone.

"But, Mum, who exactly is this woman; what is her name?"

"Well, that's part of the problem, son," his mother said. "She's the Lady Emily Gascoigne-Ridley."

"You mean … Cousin Ernest's mother?"

"No, not his mother, his aunt; he's her nephew. He's had to look after Lady Emily, since her husband died – her own daughter apparently threw her out of her house; God knows what she must have done. Monica – the daughter – is a very decent girl, indeed."

Annie shook her head. "Whatever! The fact is, Ernest asked Aunt Benedicta for help, and *she* has asked me to look after Emily, while she's here in the village."

"But that's not going to be difficult, is it Mum? I mean, she must be an old lady; she most probably just knits and crochets, all day …" The boy stared at his mother. "Why are you laughing?"

"Son, once you've met the Lady Emily, you'll realise how funny that remark was! She's only about forty-five, dresses like a film star, is fabulously wealthy – and, I mean fabulously – and is also a red-hot Socialist.

"She is coming here to convert the community into voting for a Communist Government."

"Here? In Bexford North?"

"Believe it or not, yes."

"But, nobody here votes Socialist, not even the labourers from the Quarry area."

"Well, they haven't met our Emily yet. God knows what they'll do when that actually happens; probably tar and feather her.

"However," Annie stood up, "I've got to go to the pub and see Mr and Mrs Jones – they don't know what they're in for. Get yourself a cup of tea, Billy and don't overdo the study, promise me."

As Billy promised, Annie tidied herself and set out for The Sheridan Inn. It was the only place where one could stay in the tiny village.

CHAPTER 2

"Yes, Miss Anne," the publican exclaimed happily, "your relative is arriving from Sydney tomorrow morning, after Church. She phoned me earlier today." Joe Jones and his wife Biddy were seated at the kitchen table, in the pub, with Annie.

"The Lady Emily Gascoigne-Ridley? I can't seem to place her, somehow, Miss Anne. What about you, Biddy?"

"No, Joe," his wife answered. "I think she may have visited when we both worked at the Big House, but then, I wouldn't have seen her, would I, in the kitchen? But you might have."

Biddy suddenly sat up straight. "Wait a minute!" she cried excitedly. "She's not the one that comes from up past The Junction, on the steam-train line – you know, from the north – is she? I saw that one and didn't like her, nor did my Lady."

"No, Biddy," Joe answered. "This one comes from Sydney, Vaucluse, I think she said. That's only about an hour from here, so she'd get the electric train. She said she's leaving her big car at home to aid the war effort."

Mrs Jones had insisted on making a fresh pot of tea when Annie arrived, and now went to refill her cup.

"No more, thank you Biddy," Annie said, "that was delicious. Now Mr Jones and Biddy, this is difficult for me but I have to tell you something unpleasant."

The elderly publican and his wife were surprised; they thought that their friend of many years had just dropped in for a visit and a chat.

They had known Annie since she was a little girl growing up at the Big House – now the Convalescent Hospital for soldiers – where they had been butler and cook to Annie's mother, the Lady Mary Sheridan. They still called Annie by her maiden name – which always amused her. She loved this elderly hard-working couple, and was genuinely upset that one of her family could, more than likely, cause them grief.

"I was hoping Mr Jones, that you might remember Emily," Annie explained, "as I was taking the coward's way out. You would have known all about her, without me having to tell you."

The landlord and his wife began to look alarmed.

"Whatever's the matter with the lady?" Biddy asked. "Is she sick or something?"

"Would you tell me how long she is booked in for?" Annie asked, avoiding the question.

"Three months," Jim answered immediately, "and the same for her companion."

"Her *companion*?"

"Yes, a Russian lady, a Miss Tanya Illich …"

"*Dear God!*"

"Yes, and they've taken three rooms: two bedrooms, and wanted one turned into a sitting room, which we've done." Jim moved his bulk into a more comfortable position. "And I don't have to tell you, Miss Anne, that to get two full boarders, and to let three rooms here in the middle of winter, is a godsend to us. The winters are so severe here we're usually empty until spring."

"Believe me, I *do* understand how wonderful that is for you!" Annie gently replied. "You know well I'm as poor as a church mouse myself, so I certainly do realise how great it is for you to have paying guests, in winter, and for such a long period. I would to God that my relative was a better guest for you to have."

"But, what exactly is wrong with her?" Joe Jones was mystified; Annie Watson's all encompassing kindness was legendary in the village… and to speak badly of someone!

"She's a very difficult woman. I know it sounds mad, but she seems only to get pleasure out of causing other people pain. I was so troubled when Mother Benedicta informed me she was coming here, that I had to come to warn you.

"Look, just be careful of Lady Emily. And," Annie added firmly, "whatever you are charging, *double* it. Emily is stinking rich; she'll have you running as you've never had to before, with her demands, so make her pay for it.

"As for the companion, that's new to me, but I'm scared stiff now I hear she's a Russian person…"

"Good Heavens! Why?"

"Because the Lady Emily is now a red-hot communist and has chosen this village to see if she – and, obviously her companion – can convert the whole place to the Socialist cause."

"My dear Miss Anne!" Jim and his wife were scandalised. "You can't be serious? Here? Why it's plain ridiculous. Is the lady crazy or something?"

"Unfortunately, no. Why is she doing this? Simply because she's bored; her long suffering husband is dead, and she doesn't know what to do with herself," Annie's mobile face registered disgust, "and she has so much money, she decided to use it, to try to turn this place into a showplace for the victory of the proletariat."

"Dear God!" Joe Jones had risen, but now slumped back in his chair. "But it doesn't make sense. She's a very wealthy woman; what's she doing with Socialism?"

"Unfortunately, Mr Jones, it's usually those who have too much money, who are in the forefront of the movement."

Annie pondered for a moment. "I don't imagine, for one moment, that Lady Emily would dream of losing one penny of her *own* fortune, or, one fraction of her *prestige*, to actually help the working classes. It's a great pity she's never had to work in her life – if she had, she might have found it not quite the rosy picture she imagines it is."

Annie stood up. "Look, Mr Jones, Biddy, you've been my close friends all my life. I hate to tell you these things about anyone – especially one of the family. I'm so sorry that you're going to be burdened by my tiresome relative.

"I'm happy that you have lodgers for the winter, but I simply beg of you to be careful with this lady. Nothing will suit her; she will want everything changed, she will complain sweetly, about every-thing. If you want my advice, don't give in to her in *anything at all*, or else, she'll walk all over you.

"Now, I've got to get back for Billy's lunch. I'll be here after Mass tomorrow morning, to greet this woman – she *is* a relation; I can't pretend she isn't – but if you get into any real trouble with her, just ring me.

"I'm sorry to tell you these things, but, in justice, I felt I had to warn you. Just don't let her upset you. Be on your guard from the beginning, that's all I can advise you to do." Annie shook hands with Mr Jones, kissed Biddy, and hurried back to prepare lunch for her son.

Back at the pub, Joe Jones looked at his wife.

"Biddy," he said solemnly, "if it had been anyone, but Miss Anne, I'd say they were crazy; the noble lady sounded a very nice lady indeed, on the phone, but Miss Anne …"

"You know, Joe, as well as I do, that Miss Anne never makes up stories; if she says this lady is trouble, then believe me, she must be."

"Exactly my own thoughts, old lady," growled Jim. "Well, what can we do? We've accepted the booking."

"Exactly what Miss Anne said: keep on our toes, and be on the lookout for any trouble – that's all we can do – for better or worse, we're stuck with the Lady Emily now."

CHAPTER 3

At ten thirty Sunday morning the Watson family were walking slowly towards the pub to greet their relative. Sam, Annie's husband, had cried off saying he had important work to do down in the gully behind the house.

That was nonsense, of course, but Annie was secretly relieved – it was one fewer for Emily to attack.

Annie was feeling very smart. She had dressed with extra care for Mass that morning, and had actually worn her very best frock – the only good one left. This dress had been put aside for a really big occasion; she had no coupons left for any more – nor money, if it came to that.

Annie cast a sideways look at her daughter, the lovely Penelope, looking beautiful, as usual, and wearing restrained makeup, which was a relief. However, poor Billy looked dreadful; he had grown so fast that his best suit was now too short in the trouser legs, and in the sleeves of the jacket. No matter how far Annie had managed to let down the legs and the sleeves, as well as the braces that held the pants up, the cuffs still didn't come to his ankles.

She bit her lips in frustration. He would be a target for that woman and, no matter what resolutions she had made, sparks would fly if Emily started in on Billy! But what can I do about his clothes? I have no coupons left for a new suit; not even Sam's suits are of any use – Billy's a head taller than Sam anyway.

Penelope was looking forward to meeting this relative; a cousin of some sort. She was happily conscious of how good she looked, and expected the admiration that she usually received. She was also aware that this cousin was an important lady; *and* she had a title! *George's family will be impressed with that,* she thought happily.

A taxi was driving away as the Watson family arrived at the old pub; the landlord and his wife were welcoming Lady Emily, and her companion. The two guests were surrounded by several large suitcases and hat boxes.

Lady Emily Gascoigne-Ridley had her back to the entrance and the Watsons heard her speaking as they climbed the steps.

"And of course, Mr Jones and Mrs Jones – dear, old faithful retainers! How sweet to find that today! So rare! So feudal! Such fidelity! And now with this quaint little old public house, too! So sweet!

"Now, you must promise me that you will not make any special efforts for me just because I'm part of the family you both served, so faithfully, for so many years – and because I am related to the dearly loved Lady Sheridan …" she heard people behind her, and turning, saw Annie.

Lady Emily's companion turned also, nodded slightly, and leaving her friend, went up the stairs.

"And this makes my morning complete!" Lady Emily advanced on Annie, who dutifully offered her cheek to be kissed.

Emily's shrewd eyes swept over Annie's clothes. "Ah! I'm so glad, dear Annie, that you didn't bother to dress to meet me; 'no formality' that's my motto." She smiled graciously, and gave an amused, tinkling laugh.

Annie drew in her breath sharply.

"No, Emily, I've just come straight from the cow shed, so I didn't bother to change; I mean, why bother to dress? It was only to meet you."

Lady Emily's beautiful wide-open eyes narrowed for a second, then opened wide again, as she let loose a peal of musical laughter. Penelope and Billy looked in bewilderment at their mother, aghast at her totally unexpected rudeness. Penny rushed into speech.

"Lady Emily, I'm Penelope," she smiled and held out her hand. "I don't think we've ever had the pleasure of meeting before, and this is my brother, Bil … er … William."

Lady Emily's cleverly made-up face smiled her sweetest smile at the beautiful girl. Penny, in turn, thought that this middle-aged woman was one of the prettiest she had ever seen – pansy eyes, heart-shaped face, beautiful skin, lovely golden hair, and such a clever use of wonderful makeup! Lady Emily took Penny's hand, and her eyes actually misted over.

"Ah, Penelope, you cannot believe how I've longed to meet you – and your brother, of course; I've heard of him from my nephew, Ernest." Lady Emily then fluttered her hands, in a helpless manner. "And, I wanted to ask you something really important. Now, do tell me, my dear child, are you really serious about George McKenzie?"

"I beg your pardon, Lady Emily? I do not understand. You know the McKenzies?"

Another tinkling laugh. "Of course, I do, dear. I was here last week, and I called on all the large houses – I thought it would save your dear mother the time, as she wouldn't then have to cart me around introducing me – such a bore for her, and with nothing to wear, poor thing – but, tell me, are you serious? About George, I mean."

Penny was confused; everything was happening too fast for her. "Yes, I am!" she answered honestly.

Lady Emily's pretty, pampered face, immediately creased in worried lines.

"Oh dear! Then you know all about Ruby then? You don't mind; it doesn't worry you, dear?"

"Ruby, Lady Emily? Who is Ruby? I don't understand what you mean."

Lady Emily took Penny's hand again and patted it gently. "Perhaps it's best you don't know, dear. Let's not say another word about it – no, not another word, you dear child." She deliberately turned to Billy.

"My goodness, William, I didn't know you were so tall. Of course, the Sheridans were all tall – that must be it. Ernest told me of all your studies, and your tutor … A Doctor … Harold, something."

"Dr Harold Scott, Lady Emily," Billy answered. "We get on fine; he's a tremendous chap. He's a brilliant teacher and I like him a lot."

Lady Emily turned troubled eyes on the boy. "Oh, you do? Oh dear! That's a real pity! Yes, I'm sure he is a wonderful teacher, but it's such a shame … tragedy really, about his past, isn't it? But I'm sure your parents have arranged for proper *supervision* when you are both *alone*."

Lady Emily gave her musical laugh. "I think it is better we don't talk about that part of Harold's life any more, don't you?"

Billy was confused; he didn't understand what his relative was talking about. However, he *was* aware that his mother was ready to explode with fury, so was relieved when there was an interruption.

The tall young woman with hair cut short in a man's style, dressed in a severe, grey, suit-coat and skirt, but with a man's tie, came back down the stairs to join her patroness. The woman was decidedly plain compared to the chocolate-box prettiness of Lady Emily, but could have been pretty had she taken some care with her appearance.

Billy, as usual, with perfect manners, immediately said: "I beg your pardon, Lady Emily, but we haven't yet met your companion."

Lady Emily turned and gave an amused laugh, drawing her arm through that of the young woman.

"And this is my dearest friend – and *accomplice*," another laugh, "Miss Tanya Illich. Tanya, these are my," she smiled, in an intimate, amused, confiding manner, "my *relations*."

Annie and Penny greeted the stranger, who nodded and bowed,

but said nothing. Billy thinking that the Russian woman did not speak English, spoke to her in French – he knew that many Russians spoke French.

Billy spoke, quickly and fluently, welcoming Miss Illich to the area and wishing her a pleasant winter. Miss Illich stared uncomprehendingly at Billy, her eyes wide with astonishment. After an embarrassing silence, she bowed, and said: "Da!"

Fortunately for everyone, Betty Fletcher, the pretty young barmaid, joined the landlord and his wife in the hall. Lady Emily tried to rescue the situation by speaking immediately to the barmaid.

"Oh, Mr Jones, this is the hotel worker, isn't it?"

Mr Jones was relieved to be asked a question he could answer simply.

"Yes, my Lady, it is. It's our Betty."

"Oh, Betty," cried Lady Emily, "just take this luggage up to our rooms, dear."

Betty stood firmly in front of the hotel guests. "I think you are labouring under a misapprehension. I am *not* the hotel porter; we don't have one here. So, if you want all your luggage taken upstairs, then I'm sorry to say the only way that will happen, is if you carry them up yourself."

Miss Illich's face turned red with fury. She spoke angrily in a thick accent.

"Mind your tongue, woman. This is the Lady Emily Gascoigne-Ridley."

"Really," Betty replied, completely unperturbed. "I have no intention of calling this guest by that ridiculous title. I have carefully studied the pamphlet you left last week. You wouldn't have known, but I'm a bolshie myself, so I don't believe in titles either. I'll be calling her 'Comrade Emily,' as one member of the proletariat, to another."

Betty completed the insult by coming to Annie and kissing her.

"How lovely *you* look, Mrs Watson, and what a beautiful frock! You look what you are – a *real* lady. And Penny, too. Such a beautiful girl – we're all jealous of Penny; should be a film star, we think." Betty winked at Billy. "And Billy! Looks like you'll just have to speak plain English – and very *simple* English at that, Billy – to our 'Russian' guest, who is as Russian as I am."

Betty laughed. "Her real name is Ethel Sparks; I recognized her the moment I saw her; we were in the same third grade in Primary School." After delivering this bombshell, Betty laughed heartily, took the bewildered Mr and Mrs Jones' arms and led them back inside the hotel.

There was a deathly silence in the hall; Annie seized the moment, made some polite noises, and hustled her family away from the pub as quickly as she could.

***

As soon as Annie came through the back door of her home, she picked up a pottery article from the sink without looking, and threw it as hard as she could at the furthest wall, where it shattered into a thousand pieces.

She looked at the resultant remains, scattered all over the floor, with satisfaction.

"Good, I feel better already." Taking off her gloves and hat, she spoke sharply to Penelope and Billy. "Put the kettle on, Penny, while I take this good frock off, and Billy, you get out of that suit – it's pretty dreadful, but it's the only one you've got."

Annie moved towards her bedroom, but then noticed Penny's face crumpling. "And now, young lady, what's the matter with you? Haven't we had enough drama for one morning?"

"What did she mean about 'Ruby'? *Who* is Ruby?"

"I tried to tell you what she was like, Penny. Don't believe a word she says; she will try her best to destroy any happiness anyone has."

"But there must be something in it," Penny replied, "she could so easily be proven wrong …"

"Penny!"

"No, I'm not going to just forget it, Mum. If George is playing around with this other woman – this 'Ruby' – then he can come clean about it. We made an agreement, George and I, and I've kept my part; he has obviously lied to me! No, don't try to stop me! I'm going to see George immediately – the family would be back from church by now."

So saying, Penny rushed out the back door, which crashed to, in its usual manner. Annie sighed wearily and turned to her son.

"Be a love, dear, and make me a cup of tea."

"Of course, Mum, I will, but could I say first that Lady Emily's insinuations about Dr Scott are plain stupid."

"Of course they are, Billy."

"So why did she say that?"

"Billy," Annie raised her voice, then, closing her eyes, forced herself to remain calm, "you're an intelligent young man. Can't you see what that evil woman is doing? She's poisoning everything. Get me a blasted cup of tea; let me get this dress off, and then I'll tell you more about that relative of ours."

Annie deliberately left the room, trying desperately not to say, out aloud the awful things she was thinking about her cousin. It has all started just as I thought, she grimly reflected. *And*, she has been here last week, has she? Visiting all the large houses?

God alone knows what those good people would have confided to her, once they knew she was Lady Mary's relation and a cousin of mine. She would have half the secrets of the village by now. Merciful God, what are we to do?

Left by himself in the kitchen, Billy put the kettle on and taking a dustpan, began to collect the broken china with a resigned air, wondering if his mother actually *had* another teapot; she would be grief stricken when she realised that she had smashed her best one!

CHAPTER 4

Mr Jones, Biddy and their general factotum, Betty, were seated at the kitchen table.

"Betty, dear," said the landlord of the pub, "I don't want to complain, but why did you stop me from carrying all those things up for her ladyship?"

"Look, Mr Jones, you and Mrs Jones heard what she said to Mrs Watson! It was simply cruel. You could see that Mrs Watson had spent a great deal of time, this morning, just trying to look her best, and was wearing her one, and only, very best frock – and then to be insulted like that! And then, all those mischievous insinuations about young George!"

"There's nothing to it. I knew Ruby. She was a blonde-bombshell of a girl that George was going with, years ago, before he found out what she really was like – that she didn't have a brain in her head."

"I hope Penny won't let it break off their engagement," Biddy said.

"Penny would have more sense," stoutly declared Joe Jones.

"Want to have a bet on it, Mr Jones? I'll bet you anything you like, that Penny is, at this very moment, either over at the McKenzie place, or else on the phone to George, about Ruby." The landlord's wife was troubled about another matter.

"Betty," Mrs Jones asked, "what did Lady Emily mean about

Dr Scott? He seems a wonderful young man to me – so polite, and well-mannered – and Annie tells me he actually taught at a university, before the war."

"Mrs Jones, that awful woman – the precious Lady Emily – implied that Dr Scott was not to be trusted, sexually, to be alone with Billy."

"My God! She didn't! Is that what she meant? I had no idea." Mrs Jones was scandalised that such a subject would even be mentioned! Mr Jones was more concerned with practical issues. "Betty, do you think her ladyship is right? What do you think?"

"How do I know? Dr Scott fought valiantly in the war, and was wounded horribly; he is still being treated three times a week at the Military General Hospital up the road, where he's a patient. He is gallant, in an old-fashioned sort of way, to me at the bar – it's a bit of a relief, from the crudity of the other young blokes.

"Of course, he's a bit older than the others – about thirty, I think – and also, the fact that he's not married would be enough for *that* woman, to twist things horribly."

Joe Jones scratched his head, his face worried. "So, Betty, it seems as if Annie Watson was correct in coming to warn us, of our winter guests. It looks as if it's going to be a difficult three months."

"Perhaps she won't stay the full time," Betty suggested hopefully.

"I think she will," the landlord stated, "she paid for the entire three months, last week when she called in."

"Crikey!" Betty exclaimed. "She paid, in *advance* – that's one for the books!" She stood up. "Now, don't worry; we'll manage, as we always do – we've had some weird guests in the past. If they're rude to either of you, just leave it to me. I am a match for the ghastly Lady Emily, and her bogus *Russian*!" Betty started to laugh.

"I couldn't believe my eyes when I saw who the 'Tanya Illich' was! Ethel Sparks was the stupidest kid in the whole Primary School. She was always such a *blob* – that's how I remember her! Now, I'm off to the bar; I've got work to do – it's time to open."

As Betty passed through the hall on the way to the bar she smiled brightly at the two guests struggling up the stairs laden with heavy luggage. "Don't forget, Comrades, leave your Ration Books at the desk; lunch is at half past twelve o'clock." Whistling happily, Betty opened the bar.

Back in the kitchen, Joe and his wife shared an intimate look. "What would we do without Betty, Biddy? The more I think about it, the more it seems the best thing to do. What do you think?"

"As always, Joe, exactly as you do. I'll feel happier when it's all sealed, and signed. There won't be this worrying about whether to do it, or not – it'll be done!"

"Well, I'll see Mr George McKenzie senior this week, Biddy, and get things moving."

"Right that's settled. Now, be a dear, and get out of my kitchen; I've got to prepare lunch for her ladyship. I hope she likes stew – she'd better – for that's all we have."

***

On Monday morning, Harriet McKenzie, the wife of the local solicitor and the mother of the young barrister, George, stood on her verandah waiting for Annie Watson.

Harriet's mind was equally divided with the problem that concerned both families, and for her garden, keen gardener as she was. Her pleasant middle-aged, slightly plump, face was creased with worry lines, as she surveyed the effects of the very light frost, overnight, on her plants.

Going to be a hard winter, she thought, if we have frosts as early as this; winter is only beginning. Perhaps I could cover those stock plants with hessian cloth, until they are stronger? The garden gate clicked, and Annie came through the garden to the house.

"Good morning, Harriet," she greeted the older woman, "your garden is as lovely as ever; I love it more each time I see it – winter or summer it's a patch of loveliness, in a horrible war. I always think of it like that. Those wall flowers did well, mine were useless." Annie bounded up the steps and kissed her old friend on the cheek.

"I love the garden too much I think, Annie," admitted Harriet. "Do you know it's like a drug addiction; I can't see a weed, without wanting to pull it out. I often find myself doing it in other people's gardens!

"I was talking to Amelia Tatley the other day, and without thinking, I saw a nasty onion weed and immediately dealt with it. Amelia was not pleased. She said," Harriet's face assumed an outraged expression, "'I'll have you know, Harriet, that although I am an old woman, I'm still perfectly capable of dealing with my own weeds' – that put me in my place!"

Both women laughed, as Harriet took Annie inside into the warmth of the morning room, then bustled out to the kitchen to make tea. As Harriet was busy preparing the tea things, Annie remembered to check on one of their joint activities.

"Harriet, I did remember to tell you and the other ladies, that Major Waters at the Convalescent Hospital, asked that the ladies' group not visit there for three weeks, didn't I?"

"You did, Annie; I've told all the others. Apparently they're renovating the old ballroom, which we use. There's nowhere else we can use, but it's only for three weeks though; we're to go back after that, so they still want us apparently."

"Well, it's nice to know that the medical bods still think we're doing something right, with our craft activities.

"Actually, Harriet, I'm secretly glad. I'm so far behind with planting seeds in the veggie garden, for the winter that I'm starting to get seriously worried. It's all this business with my relative …" her voice trailed off.

Harriet was relieved that Annie had broached the subject first. "Well, I don't know what to do, Annie," Harriet confided. "Young George had a face like thunder last night, and rushed off to work this morning, without even saying good morning. It must have been a terrible argument; please God it doesn't break off the engagement."

"I can't really help, either, Harriet," Annie replied, her face serious and troubled. "Penny came back last night, refused to eat, rushed to her room, slammed the door and I heard crying, which seemed to go on for hours. I tried to get to her, but the wretched girl had locked the door."

"Oh dear! It looks bad, doesn't it?"

"And," continued Annie, "this morning, she ate no breakfast and rushed off to work without a word. Her face was ashen. I'll not be the slightest bit surprised to receive a call from that dreadful woman who owns the shop, to tell me that Penny has fainted." Annie reached out and patted her friend's hand. "Harriet, I'm sorry, but I did notice that the ring was not on her finger."

"Oh then, it's worse than I feared. The engagement *is* broken!"

"Well, it seems like it at the moment. But, Harriet, remember she's a young, silly, girl; it's quite on the cards that the engagement will be on again tomorrow. Let's not rush our fences."

"But I know young George," groaned Harriet, "he's as stubborn as a mule. If he's in the wrong, it'll take an earthquake to make him say he is!" Harriet dabbed at her eyes with her handkerchief.

"And his father and I were so happy about the engagement. Nothing could have given us greater pleasure than to see your Penny and our young George, man and wife. A few years ago, I was terrified about a young woman ..."

"Would her name have been Ruby by any chance, Harriet?"

"How on earth did you know that, Annie?"

"That vicious relative of mine, the grand Lady Emily Gas-coigne-Ridley, told Penelope about Ruby when we met at the pub yesterday. Penny would never have known about this Ruby – whoever she is, or *was* – if it hadn't been for that wretched woman."

"Oh dear, then it's all my fault," Harriet began to cry. "Lady Emily called here last week, and I was so pleased to receive a visit from someone, who told me she was related to our beloved Lady Mary, to you also.

"She asked so many questions, and said she was coming to live here for the winter, and wanted to know all about everyone – so that she would fit in better."

Annie frowned. "And she asked you all about young George, his flirtations growing up, your worries about them and you came out with the Ruby story …"

"That's exactly what happened, Annie. Lady Emily was so sympathetic and interested, and with young George being our only child, naturally I cannot help talking about him … Anyway, I did tell that woman about his affair with Ruby, a hideous peroxide blonde, vulgar, uncouth, and utterly brainless.

"My George and I were absolutely terrified that young George would marry that woman and we'd be stuck with her … but more importantly, *he'd* be stuck with her, for the rest of his life! Oh, it was a dreadful period in our lives."

"How did it end, Harriet?"

"Fortunately, young George took Ruby to a Law Society social function in his Chambers, and there were important judges, barristers and other *very, very* wealthy people there.

"Well, Ruby took the eye of an elderly judge, rich as Croesus, so she ditched George, and became the mistress of the judge – I think the old fool married her, later on."

Both women started to laugh at the same time.

"Oh, it's all so ridiculous!" Annie cried. "I feel like taking a strap to Penny. Does she think, the idiot girl, George has never looked at another girl, before they got together? Oh, girls are so stupid!"

"And George is no better," declared Harriet. "Whoever said that youth and strength should be reserved for the old, was completely correct. Is there anything we can do, Annie?"

"Well, I'll certainly try to talk sense to Penny. Perhaps though, it might be wise to let it simmer for a few days. But, Harriet, forgive me for asking, but would you tell me whether you shared any other serious confidences with my terrible relative, the Lady Emily?"

Harriet looked stricken. "Well, she asked me about my neighbour Florence Armitage and ..."

Annie's face twisted in anguish. "Harriet, you *didn't*!"

"I'm afraid I did! I was saying what a wonderful woman Florence is and how splendid it is that she has her husband home with her from the war, for a couple more weeks after his terrible illness – and what a *changed* woman, she now is ..."

"Oh my God, Harriet, you've done it now! I'll have to see Florence and Stephen Armitage to warn them about Lady Emily. Oh, it's my fault ... I should never have let Mother Benedicta talk me into being nice to that terrible woman ... Her own daughter had to turn her out of her house ..."

"She didn't!"

"She did! Monica, Lady Emily's daughter, rang me about it. She said that it was either: try to save her marriage, or put her mother out of the house. And, as Lady Emily is fabulously wealthy, it was not a case of abandoning her – she could afford to live in the best hotels for the rest of her life.

"Monica has a good marriage, a very decent husband and three children, so she made the decision in favour of them – as she should."

"What an extraordinary woman Lady Emily must be; yet so pleasant on the surface!"

"That basically is the problem. It's a lesson, Harriet; never trust anyone who is all sweetness and light. She's even caused trouble with Billy's tutor, the soldier, ex-university, teacher ..."

"No! Dr Scott is a charming and erudite, man. My George thinks he's one of the finest chaps he's met."

"Well, already Lady Emily has suggested that he's a sexual predator and that Billy is his target."

"You are joking!"

"Would to God I were, Harriet. She brought it up in public

yesterday morning, when she ruined Penny's day. She spoke about something in Dr Scott's past."

"Good God, the woman is evil!"

"That's exactly what she is. And, what's more, as I was coming here this morning, I saw her coming out of the empty Fish shop – that's where Dr Scott teaches Billy; Emily had been talking to the tutor alone; Billy had not yet arrived.

"I'm frankly terrified of what she could have been saying to Harry Scott. If she's responsible for Dr Scott being removed from tutoring Billy, I'll do something drastic to that poisonous woman, also to her bogus Russian companion."

"Bogus?"

"Yes, didn't you know? Betty Fletcher ripped the disguise from Miss Tanya Illich by announcing her real name and nationality. She's Australian; she's a Miss Ethel Sparks. Betty and Tanya were in Primary School together. She's utterly bogus!"

Annie put down her cup. "Harriet, we've been friends all my life. Tell me, please dear, is there anything else I should know about your conversation with Lady Emily – if I know, then I might be able to avert some disaster, or unhappiness."

"Yes, I understand. She asked a lot of questions about Miss Tatley: where she taught, whether she was promoted, who were her parents.

"Then she was very interested – now I come to think of it – in Joan Hennessy, and asked me about her boy-friend, Dan Kelly, from the dairy; I told her how proud we were of Joan, and her wonderful VAD work.

"She also asked about Thelma and Edward Kemp – whether I thought he was a good doctor? How long had he been here? Where was Thelma nursing when she married Edward?

"Really, Annie," Harriet looked surprised and angry, "when I think of all the things she *did* ask me, it was very 'nosy'. How could I not have recognised I was being 'pumped'? She was simply using me! How utterly disgusting!"

Harriet's outrage turned to anguish. "But, Annie, God help me, what damage have I done to my best friends and neighbours? Oh, God forgive me; I didn't intend to give away people's secrets – I never realised I was doing so!"

"Harriet, stop it! It's my family that has caused all this. Although, I hasten to add, Emily is only related by marriage – that's some salve to my pride. Anyhow, you are utterly and completely innocent, and one of the best women I've ever known. We've got to work out a method of beating this woman at her own game."

Annie stood up. "I'll go now, Harriet; thank you for being so frank. I'll see if something can be done for Florence and Stephen – what they have now, is too priceless to lose, and Stephen goes back to war in a couple of weeks.

"And, finally, I beg of you, don't spend the rest of the day beating your breast: you're not the first person to be gulled by Emily. I poured out my heart to her, many years ago, only to find my confidences repeated in a gossip column she was writing at the time, for a Sydney newspaper – she was using me for copy!"

Annie kissed Harriet and hurried to the imposing mansion of Florence and Stephen Armitage.

Annie heard the sound of a man digging and whistling, as she entered the Armitage garden. She found Stephen in the midst of his wonderful garden, now fully restored to its former beauty by the work done during the past three months.

When Stephen became aware of a visitor he made a hurried attempt to pull his shirt on, but when he saw that it was Annie, he laughed and left it where it was. Annie also laughed.

"Yes, it's only me! No need to pretend with me, Stephen Armitage!" She came forward and shook the proffered hand. "Stephen, you look marvellous. I can't get over it! Three months ago I thought you would never recover – honestly I did, and now, you look the picture of health."

"Physically and *mentally*," Stephen laughed. Annie understood what he meant. Three months ago, Stephen had been admitted to the, now-called, 'Convalescent' Hospital – then called the 'Mental' Hospital – suffering from severe trauma-related illness.

It had only been through the machinations of Annie, and her powerful relations, that Stephen had been permitted, by the army, to be given a three months respite period, at his own home, before he returned to the war.

Then, it had been through the loving and devoted care of his wife, Florence, that Stephen was now well again and he was thrilled not only with his recovery, but with the renewed state of their marriage.

It was this awareness of the true happiness both husband and wife had found, which caused Annie severe distress now, with the topic she had to broach.

Annie had a very mobile face and Stephen quickly saw that Annie had not come for a social chat.

"Annie, dear, what's the matter? Out with it; I know there's something wrong."

"There is, Stephen, and it doesn't make it any easier for me to bring trouble to you and Florence – when it has been caused by my own relative."

To her surprise, Stephen started to laugh. "You wouldn't be talking about the sweet little old Lady Emily, would you?"

"Yes," admitted Annie miserably, then was suddenly aware of the reaction of Stephen. "But, Stephen, why are you *laughing*?"

"Because, whatever you were going to tell me, I know already."
Annie gasped. "You do?"

"Yes, Annie, I do. The Lady Emily came to me, and thought it *her duty, as a friend of yours*, to let me know all the details!"

"Oh, dear God! And using my *name*! What did you say to her? She needs her pampered face slapped!"

"I laughed in her face; she was furious!"

"You weren't angry? Oh, I've been in torment, ever since I heard from poor Harriet, who's in agony at what she unwittingly let out of the bag."

"Tell her not to worry. You see, Annie, right at the beginning of my time at home, Florence was severely troubled about something and I begged her to tell me; whatever it was, it wouldn't make the slightest difference to me. And I meant that Annie. There's never ever been another woman than Florence, for me, in my life. She is, and always will be, my 'Florrie'. There'll never be anybody else."

"And Florrie told you?"

"Everything."

Annie paused, trying to think of a delicate way of saying the next thing, but Stephen anticipated her. "And, it hasn't made the slightest bit of difference to me. I'm no angel myself. Anyhow, these three months have been the happiest of my entire life, and I humbly think that goes for Florence as well."

A female voice came from behind some trees in the garden. "And you'd be absolutely right, Stephen! I've not only been truly happy, for the first time in my life – but I have something to tell you."

Annie was embarrassed. "Dearest Florrie, I only heard from Harriet McKenzie today that she had, without realising it, revealed things to that horrible woman, Lady Emily.

"I was trying to get here in time, to tell Stephen, not to believe anything that woman told him."

Florence came forward and hugged her close friend. "Annie, I might have known that you'd be trying to fix things up. But, the glorious thing is, there's *nothing* to fix up." Florence went to her husband and, comically, pretended to feel his forehead and take his pulse. Stephen laughed.

"What on earth are you up to now, Flossie?"

"Tell me, Stephen do you feel really and truly well? I mean, really strong?"

"Of course, I do. What do you mean?"

"Well, you'll never believe this, after all our years of trying." Florence took Stephen's hand in hers. "Stephen, I'm *pregnant*. Dr Kemp is certain now; he wasn't before. Stephen, at last, I'm pregnant!" Stephen was staring at his wife, his eyes dazed with shock.

"Flossie, Flossie …" he murmured taking his wife in his arms. "This is the greatest gift God could ever have given us. I can't believe it … I'm forty-one …"

"And I'm thirty-eight." Her eyes became tragic; she turned to Annie, for comfort. "Annie, I'll be all right won't I? I'm not too old, am I? God couldn't take away my baby now after giving it to me, could He? We always wanted a child so much, and I was never able to conceive before. It's a miracle, an absolute miracle!"

Annie took her friend in her arms. "Flossie, this is the best news I could ever have received. Of course, it's a little unusual to have a first baby so late but certainly not all that unusual.

"You're a strong, healthy woman, and if you do exactly as Dr Kemp tells you, during the pregnancy, I'm sure you'll be fine."

"I have to tell you, Annie," confided Florence, "as soon as I found out, I rang Mother Benedicta and told her. She has written my intentions on the list pinned to the chapel door for the nuns, so they'll be praying for me, for the entire time."

"And believe me, so shall I," declared Annie. "After all the trouble Lady Emily has caused, thanks be to God it failed to harm you, as it has already harmed others."

Stephen looked serious. "Annie, somehow or other, we've got to stop that woman. She is evil."

Annie nodded, "*How* is the problem and before something terrible happens – as a result of her mischief."

CHAPTER 5

While Annie was talking to Harriet McKenzie, Dr Scott had just seated himself at a large table in the empty fish shop, with Billy Watson. On the table were a pile of books and papers.

Mr Tanby, the butcher, who owned this shop, as well as his own next door, had popped in to see if everything was all right – as he did most mornings. The empty shop had been a godsend to Billy. He needed somewhere quiet and private for his lessons, and the Watson's house was too small to have any quiet corners. Mr Tanby had come to the rescue and let the soldier-tutor and Billy have the empty shop for nothing; the only condition being, that they swept the floor and kept it tidy.

Harry Scott was thirty years old, thin and weary-looking, his sensitive face looking younger than his years. His hair was brown and he was often troubled at its inclination to burst into curls when it rained. He kept it severely in control with brilliantine.

His fingers were long and beautifully shaped. He actually looked more like the popular conception of a violinist than an academic. His manner was often preoccupied and distant, but for those who managed to get close to him, he had a warmth of manner and a surprisingly wonderful, sense of humour.

He did have one thing not usually found in young men: he had enormous *compassion*. When asked by his friend, Dr Ernest Gascoigne-Ridley, whether he would undertake the tutoring of this unusual Watson boy, he was reluctant to do so. It was only after meeting both Billy and his mother, that Scott had found an affinity with both, that he rarely found with other people.

He liked and respected Billy, and was constantly amazed how this young boy had come to terms with his terrible cardiac condition, without any histrionics, or self-pity concerning the future.

Harry Scott and Billy had now been studying for one month and got along famously. Billy found that this tutor had the gift of genius in making everything they studied, a vital and interesting, experience. He was a gifted teacher and Billy was a remarkable student.

To have a student preparing for the matriculation examination for University entrance and scholarship, at the age of fifteen, and one who *spoke* three languages, could *read* and understand Latin, and was willing, at Scott's urging, to undertake the onerous task of learning yet another language – Basic Elementary Greek; this was something that had never happened to the tutor before. He doubted if it ever would happen again.

The boy had a good grounding in Latin already, from his mother; Scott hoped that would compensate, for any deficiency in Greek, in the total marks.

When Billy had arrived on Monday morning with his usual cheerful enthusiasm, he noticed that the atmosphere was different. Dr Scott returned Billy's greeting, but looked distressed; he seemed to have difficulty looking Billy straight in the eye. He covered his obvious embarrassment with a cloak of severity; demanding to see immediately the homework that he had ordered done.

Billy handed over his work, happily conscious that he had completed all that had been asked of him, but being a sensitive and perceptive lad, was worried that he had somehow offended his teacher.

There was silence as the tutor read through the papers Billy had done. When it was finished, Harry Scott looked up, but not directly *at* Billy.

"Billy," he began, his voice cold and emotionless, "I'm sorry but I have to take a break from this work for a while." Billy's face had gone white, and the tutor's voice faltered.

"Sir, have I done something wrong? Have I offended you? Please tell me anything that was wrong. I don't think I could bear it, if you were angry with me – I truly have tried to do the best I could …"

Dr Scott held up his hand to stop the flow. This time he actually looked at Billy directly.

"Please stop Billy," he entreated, his voice breaking. "There is nothing you have done wrongly. You have been perhaps the best student I have ever had. What has happened has nothing whatever to do with you. But, I think I have to go away for a while …"

There was a wail of despair from his student.

"Oh, no, please don't say that! This has been the greatest thing that has ever happened to me in my life; both my mother and I think you are the greatest teacher in Australia. If I get through the matriculation exam it will be entirely because of you …"

"Please, don't make it harder for me, Billy, than it already is, I beg of you as … as … a friend, not your teacher. I have …"

"Is something wrong, Dr Scott? Why not speak to my mother? She pretty scatty, but she's super intelligent and often comes up with the most surprising answers to people's problems."

Dr Scott smiled briefly. He thought the eccentric Annie Watson was everything that Billy said, but also was one of the kindest women he had ever met.

"Perhaps I will do that, Billy," he agreed wearily, "but I need to think something out clearly. I'm going back to the hospital now and I've written out a programme for you to go on with …"

"But, how long …?"

"At the moment, I'm sorry, but I just don't know." Dr Scott stood up. "Lock the door when you leave, Billy, Mr Tanby is relying on us to do that … and," he reached across to take the boy's hand, then pulled back sharply, "I'll give you a phone call, when we can start again."

He could not bear seeing the distraught look on the boy's face, so gathered up his things quickly and left the shop. By the time Billy had done the same, he saw his teacher already well along the road, leading to the big military hospital – he was almost running.

It was a well-nigh desperate Billy who trudged back to his home, hoping that his mother would soon be back from her visits.

***

Annie, hurrying home after leaving the Armitage house, was unaware she had walked past Laura Hennessy leaning over her gate. Laura called after her: "Annie, Annie Watson."

Annie turned, and then laughed.

"Here I am, Laura, stupid as usual. Lost in my own thoughts I didn't even see you. Did you want me?"

"Well, I did, dear. Could you spare a minute?"

"Of course, but I don't have a lot of time, Laura; could we talk here?" Annie studied her friend's face and noticed the tell-tale signs of worry and anxiety. Laura was Annie's age, and a widow with one child, a daughter, Joan. Annie was very fond of the Hennessys.

"It's Joan," Laura began. Annie had a sinking feeling in her stomach. "Well, Joan *and* Dan Kelly."

"Oh, dear! Laura, don't tell me there's trouble between the two of them. I thought it was an excellent match and I've been praying that the engagement would be announced soon."

"So was I, dear, so was I," Laura replied. "Yes, there's trouble. You see, someone has been speaking to Joan, and also to Dan ..."

"Don't tell me! It was the Lady Emily, wasn't it?"

"How on earth did you know that?" asked Laura surprised.

"Simply because there is hardly a person, so it seems, left in the village that that dreadful woman has not harmed in some way, already.

"And, she's only been here a few days." Annie looked sternly at her neighbour. "Laura, did that woman call here to see you last week?"

"She did, and I welcomed her as a relation of our dear Lady Mary, and of course, of you, too, Annie."

"The more I have to do with that woman, the easier I find it to believe in the snake in the Garden of Eden, as in Genesis! I suppose she asked you all kinds of questions about Joan: who was her boyfriend, where did he live, were they happy together; what work did Joan do? Where? Was Dan involved in any way, with another girl? …

"Am I on the right track?"

Laura Hennessy was staring at Annie in amazement. "How did you know? That's exactly what she did. She was so …"

"…*sympathetic and understanding, and so sweet and nice,*" Annie finished the sentence for Laura. "Laura, she's the devil incarnate. She thrives on destroying other people's happiness. She has already broken off Penny and George's engagement, and destroyed the reputation of Billy's tutor, Dr Scott …"

"No!"

"Yes, and that's why I didn't see you, dear. I've been to see poor Florence. It seems that the precious Lady Emily felt it, *her duty*, to point out to Stephen, Florence's … er … peccadilloes of the past."

"Oh, my God! That is the cruellest thing I've ever heard! What's wrong with the woman? Apparently, no one is safe! But what about my Joan and Dan, Annie? What should I do?"

"I think the first thing I must do is to speak to Hannah Kelly. Hannah is possibly the most practical and sensible woman, in this whole area. She needs to know about this – of course, she may know already. I'll phone her the moment I get back." Annie rubbed her forehead irritably, sending her wild hair flying loose from its pins.

"Laura, your daughter Joan is a sensible girl, and Dan is a fine young man – he's doing a magnificent job holding that huge dairy farm together – with just his mother and him to do all the work.

"Tell Joan all that I've told you about Lady Emily. Tell her from me, to take no notice of anything that woman says; nine-tenths of all she says is fiction – she makes it up as she goes."

"I'll do that, Annie, and thank you," Laura promised. "And, to think I have possibly ruined my daughter's happiness by talking to that woman! However, the Lady Emily will learn that won't happen again, I assure you."

Annie patted the hand on the gate, and hurried along Tully Road to her own house.

***

As Betty Fletcher deposited the heavy tray neatly onto the kitchen bench, Mrs Liveridge, the casual dish-washer and cleaner, asked tartly:

"So, Betty, do you know where the Lady Red-Shirt's been this morning?"

"No, I don't Mrs Liveridge, but I saw her and the Illich person, going out early."

"Well, I'll tell you. They've been at the Quarry, with their wretched pamphlets, visiting every house, and introducing themselves as relatives of our Lady Mary and of Mrs Watson. Everyone invited them in because of that and, before you knew it, you were being given a pile of pamphlets to read."

"Yes, I've read them, Mrs Liveridge. A load of clap-trap actually."

"That's what I thought, but I'm not much of a reader. But my Bert, *is* … And that's the trouble, Betty." Mrs Liveridge took her soapy hands out of the water and dried them quickly with a cloth.

Betty was disturbed to see that the elderly woman was in tears.

"Why, Mrs Liveridge, whatever's the matter? Are you unwell? If so, don't worry, I'll do the washing up today."

"No, dear, you're a good kind girl. No, it's those bloody pamphlets. Bert was reading them as I left … and – just between you and me, love – he's always been a bit 'bolshie' – against the Government, the upper classes, and all that."

"I suppose a lot of Australians are, Mrs Liveridge; given our history I suppose it's natural, really," Betty responded. "But I don't think we're likely to take to the street, and slaughter anyone," she laughed, then spoke seriously. "And, with this frightful war going on as if it's never going to end, there is enough slaughter already. This terrible war ..."

"But *that's* just the problem, Betty," interrupted Mrs Liveridge. "One of the pamphlets is against the war; called it a ... wait a minute ... a ... 'Struggle between two Empires' ... and that it's got nothing to do with Australia.

"And all about Russia, showing us how we should be governed; how wise they were, to keep out of the war ... and how our boys should *desert* from the Army."

"That'd not go down too well with your neighbours in the Quarry road, would it? I think there are at least four houses with boys overseas and ..."

"One boy dead and three other boys in prison camps," finished Mrs Liveridge. "So with the pamphlets, and my Bert agreeing with them, and the neighbours saying awful things to me ..." the old woman turned to Betty, who held her in her arms and let her have her cry out. A moment or two later, Mrs Liveridge apologized, blew her nose loudly, and returned to the sink.

Betty, returning to the dining room, was pondering the situation seriously: something has to be done about this terrible woman. But, what *could* be done? Her thoughts flew to her friend, Major Tim Johnson whom, she secretly hoped, could soon become something *more* than just a friend. If he comes in this afternoon for a beer, I'll talk to Tim about it, she decided.

CHAPTER 6

When Annie had finished her call to her friend, Hannah Kelly at the big dairy, and had promised to visit as soon as she could find the time, she went in search of Billy. She had noticed that the Fish shop door was closed as she returned, so Billy had to be at home somewhere.

Annie searched in the usual places dear to Billy: the old cow shed where Daisy, their old pet cow, had lived; then the little hidden area, which sported a small grave with a roughly made cross and the name 'Agnes' written on it. She remembered, with a lump in her throat, the sight of Billy and his sick, black, American soldier-friend, Louis, standing there after Agnes, Billy's very old pet hen, had been ceremoniously interred.

I wonder where Louis is now, Annie worried; it's been a full month since he was pronounced fit and well again and sent back to re-join his unit in the Pacific. God keep that good, innocent young man safe, Annie prayed; don't let him be harmed again.

And, please God, let us receive a letter from Louis soon – from, wherever he is – just so we'll know *he's safe.*

After searching the yard, calling his name, Annie began to be slightly worried. Billy was totally realistic about his illness and about the need to always let his parents know where he was at all times.

It was utterly out of character for him to just disappear like this. A sudden thought struck Annie. He could be across at the blacksmith's forge – he often fled there in moments of great anguish – and … if he's there, then there's trouble.

She hurried across the road and up the short lane beside Nan Brady's house to the forge. To her relief, she saw Billy sitting silently, in one corner of the building, while Reg the Smithy, hammered out a horse shoe on the anvil.

Annie greeted Reg Cerney, asked about his wife Susan, and their beautiful new daughter, Angela; she then beckoned silently to Billy, who rose with a sigh, and followed his mother from the forge.

"I'm sorry Mum," he said wearily, "I should've left a note saying where I'd gone, but something happened." His mother was immediately alarmed.

"You are not feeling bad, are you son?"

"No, it's nothing like that. It's Dr Scott …"

"Tell me quickly. What about Dr Scott?"

"I think he's going to give me up. I must have offended him in some way. I certainly didn't mean to, but I must have. Why else would he go away, as soon as I got to the shop this morning?"

"Billy, this is terribly important. Listen carefully. Tell me every single thing that happened when you went across to the shop this morning. Leave nothing out at all." Billy closed his eyes for a moment and then repeated all that had happened – it wasn't much really to tell.

"So, Billy, he actually went to shake your hand, then pulled back, did he?"

"Yes, I was surprised, for we always shook hands, when we were leaving each day; I thought my hands must have looked dirty, or something."

They had reached their house by this time; Billy went to his room and Annie sat at the kitchen table with her head in her hands. That woman! I knew she was up to no good, when I saw her coming out of the fish shop this morning, before Billy got there.

What has she said to Dr Scott that would drive him away? Wait a minute! She said something about 'his past' – she must know something bad about the poor man. What else? Threatened him with exposure, perhaps? Who knows?

For the love of God, doesn't this woman have any pity at all? Dr Scott's a sick man; wounded badly after serving for nearly four years in the worst battles of the war, and now this! Is no one on earth safe from that fiendish creature?

Annie sat up. It's no good guessing. I've got to find out, if he really is just ill – he could have just had a relapse; that's a possibility. I'll ring Major Waters at the Convalescent Hospital, and ask him to investigate quietly for me.

He could find out the medical state of Captain Scott from his colleagues at the big Military Hospital up the road. I must do something – Billy's whole future depends on this.

I'll have to ring Ernest Gascoigne-Ridley as well – he arranged for the tutoring. She rose wearily, from the chair and went to the phone. We say the words in our prayers: 'this vale of tears' often enough, and *easily* enough, she thought, but it seems sometimes that's all there is in life: tears!

***

Hannah Kelly, a big, raw-boned Irishwoman with a strong colour and a loud voice, put down the phone and sat at her large kitchen table.

Here's a fine kettle of fish, and no mistake! And I was so nice to that blasted woman, she remembered; nearly burst a vessel being so polite! And, for what? I was just being pumped and I didn't realise it! But what about my Dan? What has she said to Dan, or to Joan?

Would Dan tell me? If it were one of the twins – God have mercy on them, wherever they are – Hannah crossed herself quickly, screwing her eyes tight at the very thought of her baby twins, two years younger than Dan, fighting 'somewhere overseas'. This always filled her with horrendous misery ... Yes, the twins would tell me ... but Dan? I'll have to be very careful here. He's a proud man, just like his father, God rest his soul.

She went in search of her son.

Dan Kelly was a big, physically very strong, young man – strong with the endless work of the dairy; his twelve or fourteen hour days spent in all weathers, had tanned his skin dark, and had given him muscles, that made him a formidable figure. He had his father's strong pride, his mother's stubbornness and now he was in a muddle.

He wanted so desperately to talk to his mother, about the situation with Joan, and yet was secretly afraid that she would say the wrong thing, or, even laugh at him. No, that wasn't fair, she'd never laugh at him, but she might not understand, or, worse still, think that it was all true – after the business at the Big House, last year...with, Mrs Armitage!

***

Telephone call to Dr Major Ted Waters at the Convalescent Hospital:

"Yes, it's only me Doctor ... Annie Watson ... No, I'm fine, and Billy also. I have a problem; can you spare a few minutes? You can! Thank you. You know Captain Harry Scott? Yes Dr Scott ... Yes, I agree, a brilliant teacher; Billy thinks he's the greatest teacher in the world; they have been working very hard together and are great friends as well ...

"Well, I don't know whether you've heard that a relative of mine has come to stay in the village, for the winter? ... Oh, you have? *Really*! You have made the hospital out of bounds, to both her and her friend, the Russian?

"Oh, Major, I am so relieved to hear that ... No, not about the trouble she's caused you at the hospital, but because I don't need to explain about the woman. If she's caused you trouble, then you'll understand … Yes, she's mentioned, publicly, that Dr Scott has something bad in his past, and … pardon? … Yes, I do agree; she's a mischief-making, bad woman, but the damage has been done.

"It seems, Dr Scott saw Billy only for a few minutes this morning, then said that he could not continue, as something had happened.

"He left some work for Billy to do and almost ran away back to the hospital … Yes, I agree, I'm very worried about the poor man. He's been terribly ill, after being wounded so badly and he's fought for all those years of war – and now to be treated like this! …

"Well, what I thought was this: I don't know whether Dr Scott could just be having a relapse of his illness and I wondered if you could make some discreet enquiries from your colleagues, up at the General Hospital? …

"Yes, I thought you would agree to that; you can see why I am worried. If it's not just sickness, then I'm afraid for him. He's a good man; I don't care what he's done – it's most probably nothing; that dreadful woman makes up the most terrible lies about people – and I do want to help Harry Scott if I possibly can … You will? Thank you, Doctor; I knew I could count on you."

Annie put the phone down and pondered her next call. It might be possible to speak to Dr Ernest Gascoigne-Ridley, if he happens to be in his office, but if not, she could leave a message; he'd ring back when he could. She dialled the number, and spoke to his secretary.

"Really? He's actually there, Margaret? Could he give me a couple of minutes? I do know how fearfully busy the good man is and I promise you I'll not keep him. Thank you … …Ernest? Thank you for your time. I'll be brief … No, everyone is all right, and Billy is fine – well he isn't really, but that what it's all about …

"Yes, it concerns Harold Scott … No, he's been the greatest thing that's ever happened to Billy – they are doing splendidly and are great friends … Well, I'm *trying* to tell you. You see, Ernest, your Aunt, Lady Emily …

"Yes, you're right; yes, she's to blame. Ernest, she's already caused havoc here in the village: Penelope's engagement is broken, so is the Hennessy girl's, Joan, to the Kelly boy and … About Harold Scott? Ernest, be *reasonable*, I don't find this easy to talk about.

"Lady Emily implied, publicly, that there was something bad – sexually bad – in poor Dr Scott's past … Yes, she did, she's a horrible woman and I don't think I'll ever forgive Aunt Benedicta for begging me to be nice to her.

"Anyhow, the upshot of all this is that Dr Scott has thrown in the tutoring and rushed off back to the hospital, awfully upset – in a terrible state according to Billy. I've asked Dr Waters at the Convalescent Hospital to find out if Harry is just ill, or whether the reason is related to Lady Emily's insinuations …

"Billy is devastated, as you would expect. I don't know what to do …What? Are you really? You're coming to the Convalescent Hospital on Thursday? Ernest – could you also see poor Harold Scott, at the other hospital? …

"Yes, you told me he was a friend of yours, that's why I felt so happy about the situation. We have come to like the chap very much. Anyhow, you *will* see him definitely on Thursday, when you come out here? God bless you, Ernest, and thank you."

CHAPTER 7

Early Wednesday morning, Tanya Illich sat alone in the sitting room she shared with Lady Emily, relishing the silence.

She was glad to be alone for a while; free of the incessant meaningless chatter of her patroness. Lady Emily was engaged in a protracted cosmetic session, involving a face mask and cucumbers. Tanya's lips curled in contempt.

Her own face was devoid of makeup except for a slight dusting of face powder. She despised all flipperies ... and despised her patroness as well.

Tanya was under no illusions whatsoever concerning Emily's commitment to the whole Socialist movement. While to Tanya, it was a crusade in which she would happily shed her blood, if needed; to the Lady Emily, it was merely a vehicle to use to wreak her vengeance on other people, indeed, on society in general, which she believed had wronged her – how exactly, it was difficult for Tanya to understand.

Emily had never had to work in her life; had everything she could ever ask for, or even want.

Tanya secretly believed that Emily was quite paranoid, but very *useful*, indeed vital, for her own purposes, so it behoved her to be the useful, and docile, admirer, and secretary, while it lasted.

Tanya was fully aware that this Socialist 'escapade' of Lady Emily's would not last much longer. She would soon tire of it and tire of this place; it was too small for Emily – she would soon exhaust the possibilities here for venting her spleen against mankind.

But, while it lasted, she, Tanya, must try to make the best use of it.

It had certainly been a happy chance that they had met at the lecture Tanya had given. Lady Emily had been completely captivated by the vehemence of the speaker.

Having never really believed in anything herself, Tanya's utterly genuine conviction was overwhelming. Emily was immediately converted to the Cause; made it her business to meet the speaker and discovered Tanya was in need of patronage.

She immediately offered the girl the position of Companion/ Secretary, as they joined forces, to rid the world of Capitalism and to help bring about the victory of the proletariat.

Tanya often thought with gratitude of that meeting with this titled lady. She also often pondered her own upbringing, with a shudder.

An unattractive child, so shy she was thought to be stupid; forced to wear those dreadful braces on her teeth and those ghastly, thick greasy, ugly, plaits. Growing up had been worse, the attempt to be attractive, to be popular like the other girls, the longing to have a boyfriend of her own and, finally, her own ultimate despair. Then, the awakening!

It came about when she had, inadvertently, entered a Feminist Club by mistake, discovered people who offered her friendship and, with their help, she began to re-make herself. First had been the hair. The long heavy hair, was replaced by a short back and sides and then the clothes! She had been guided as to what to wear for this new person, she was becoming.

Finally: the introduction to the ideology of Russian Communism, which in the devastation of most of Europe – caused by the global war – had become, for many, the utopian ideal that Stalin had achieved in the new grouping of nations called the USSR.

France, Spain, Italy and other European countries, had groups ardently working for the great Cause, which would be the solution to remake society when this stupid war was finally over. It would 'end all wars'.

Australia, as well, had a thriving dedicated group of adherents who pursued the Cause with Evangelistic fervour. To this group, Tanya had been introduced.

The Communist Gospel had had an immediate appeal to the lonely, friendless girl; she attended courses, applied herself as never before and, with this new confidence in herself, discovered that she was becoming an excellent, public-speaker.

When the Leaders realised this, they coached her in speaking, set her to work with a Russian vocal coach, sent her on special training courses, and eventually, she had become one of the top leaders herself. To her great surprise, she was soon a regular speaker at meetings, throughout the country.

But, she was desperately poor herself; she needed money urgently. She had previously been obliged to work, part-time, as a typist and secretary, but work took up so much of her time, which should have been dedicated to the Cause.

However, it had all come right, when she met Lady Emily. Now, her work and the Cause were one and the same. And, if she did have to put up with the inane, stupid prattle of the superficial titled idiot, well, it would only be for a short time; soon, the streets of Sydney would be awash with the blood of the Revolution.

Meanwhile, she steeled herself to be the admiring, flattering, fool – that Lady Emily truly thought she actually was.

Tanya looked round the pretty room in which she was sitting. This was living! She thought with horror of her own tiny 'bed-sit' – with the use of the bathroom on the landing. She smiled grimly, as she thought of all the complaints Lady Emily continued to make about this 'dreadful hovel'; this 'degrading standard of living'; and then 'the service'! 'Merciful Heavens, the service'!

Tanya laughed quietly. To her, the place was heaven, and as a good communist she was forbidden to believe in Heaven, so this would do instead!

It was a pity that she had immediately been recognized by that awful, Betty Fletcher – who would have believed that someone *from third grade* would recognize her again? And such a nasty woman too, with a tongue on her and no mistake!

It was the only fly in the ointment, as far as Tanya was concerned.

She had worked so hard on the accent and her coaching had been excellent. Now, when she spoke, she didn't even have to remember to use the Russian accent –it just came naturally. Pity really, that she had such difficulty, with the language, but she did have a vast number of phrases by now and they had always managed to be enough so far.

Oh, well, it doesn't matter; being recognized. In a way, it makes her role more authentic. People would see that she believed so firmly in the Russian revolution, that, in her admiration, she had changed her name to be one with the revolutionaries.

And, indeed, she *had* changed it by deed-poll; no matter how they checked up on her, she was undoubtedly, *legally*, Tanya Illich.

Tanya suddenly took out her notebook. Today, 'she,' the grand lady, was going to see Major Nicholls for some reason or other – it didn't matter what, as long as she was busy – and then had said something, about consulting her solicitor in Bexford – that should keep her occupied all morning – after the beauty treatment – anyhow.

What shall I do? She wondered, then made a decision. I know, I'll continue in the Quarry area, she decided.

There were great possibilities with Bert Liveridge; also with the Firellis, the market gardeners. The Firellis were Italian, and therefore, not against the idea of Communism – after Mussolini – and they were, at the moment, furious that their menfolk had been interned, by the stupid Government, as aliens.

Tanya's lips curled in contempt: interned, even though they had been in Australia for three generations! Yes, there's good scope for propaganda there. Tanya put her notebook and pamphlets in her large handbag and decided to slip away now to the Quarry area.

She'd just leave a note for her Ladyship. That way, she wouldn't even have to speak to her at all – which would be a great bonus indeed!

Before she left the room, Tanya put on her one and only piece of jewellery that she owned, and which she wore everywhere. It was a small, but very pretty, insignificant gold, heart-shaped pendant on a thin chain. The whole ornament so unobtrusive, that most people never noticed it and that pleased her; she hated obtrusive, showy jewellery.

She had noticed, of course, but Tanya had refused to open the locket, to let Emily see inside, informing her that it was some hairs of her dead grandmother's head, and that she held them sacred.

Lady Emily had shuddered, dramatically, at the thought of wearing a dead person's hair around your neck! Tanya smiled; that had shut up the bourgeois clown! It had been given to her by a very dear friend and she had no intention of telling Emily that!

***

Annie timed her visit to Hannah Kelly for the period at the end of the morning milking and breakfast, but before the hard-working, dairywoman began her day's chores. As usual, as soon as she had arrived, Hannah had insisted on the ritual cup of tea and soon the two women were sitting in the big farmhouse kitchen.

Annie had known Hannah all her life so there was the easiness of long association in the meeting. Annie asked about the two twins overseas and shared Hannah's unfeigned anguish in the reply: 'no word at all'.

The two boys had been favourites with Annie, and she felt, as did their mother, that two babies had been sent to the slaughter.

"Hannah," Annie said, "it's about Dan that I want to talk …"

"I know, Annie. He hardly spoke this morning all the time we were working. I don't know what to do. I'm even terrified that he'll go and get drunk and be unable to do the milking; I've got no one else."

"Hannah, I've been wondering about that problem. Look, have you considered the Women's Land Army?"

"I've heard of them. It was only started last year, wasn't it?"

"Yes. I don't know what those girls are like, but they must be better than no one."

"Do you think I'd be able to get any from the authorities?"

"I'd like to know why not? First they take away your two boys, leaving only Dan and you to work the entire farm and the blasted army takes all the milk. Surely to God they must see that you can't keep going, as you are, working seven days a week, every week of the year. That's far more than those lazy, fat, politicians in the Government ever work in their lives."

"What would be the best way to go about it, Annie? Through the Milk Inspector?"

"Yes, good idea! I'm sure that wretched Milk Inspector, who gives you such a bad time, should be the one to bring it about. After all, it's in the army's own interest, that you keep producing the milk, isn't it? Speak to him about it next time he comes; it's worth a try anyway."

Annie thought what she had said and decided to amend it,

"Forget what I just said, Hannah. Don't *ask* for the Land Girls, *demand* them! They really cannot refuse. You could sort of 'hint' that if they didn't arrive within a day or two, you would be taking that long bed-rest you had been told to take by the doctor."

Hannah looked startled, then both women laughed.

"I'll do it! I'll try, anyway. It's not fair on me, but it's also not fair on poor Dan. He works from morning to night every day in the week. And now he's got this …"

"Hannah, did you manage to find out what exactly the ghastly Lady Emily said to Dan?"

"The only thing I got out of Dan was that it was something about Joan Hennessy carrying on with the soldiers, at the Red Cross Hospital at The Junction, where she works as a VAD."

"As vague as that?"

"Yes. I know it's ridiculous, but when you're twenty it only needs something like that to cause your world to collapse. And Dan is so stubborn."

"I've actually begged him to go to Joan, and ask straight out what the problem is; or whether her feelings for him, have changed, and she wants to break it off. So far, he's refused. Said that 'people must be talking about Joan' if Lady Emily, had heard of it."

"Oh, that blasted woman; she could have made it up! Can't he see that? No, I suppose he can't. Why should he? He doesn't know her. And who am I to talk? Penny and George have broken off their engagement ..."

"Oh. No, Annie, they haven't!"

"They have, Hannah, and all because of Emily's vicious tongue about some old flame of George, called Ruby, who George once knew."

"Annie," Hannah Kelly stated solemnly, "something has to be done about the lady Emily."

"I agree, but I don't know what. Mr Jones at the pub tells me she paid for the entire winter in advance."

"Good God! I've never heard of such a thing – *in advance?* She must be loaded with money."

"She is, that's the trouble. Look, Hannah ... about Dan, do you think he would listen to me if I spoke to him."

"I honestly don't know, Annie. I think it might be better to just wait a couple of days. His loneliness might break down his suspicions.

"He did so look forward to Joan coming up of a night for an hour and then walking her back home. It was the only bright thing to look forward to in the whole day, for the poor young man."

Annie nodded her understanding. "Truly, Hannah, it's not just those who go away, dressed up in uniforms, who are suffering; the ones at home, I think, have the worst job of all."

Dan came into the kitchen at that moment and the women immediately began to speak of local affairs; the Firellis were the main topic of conversation.

The Firelli family had been the Kelly's neighbours for the whole of Dan's life; he found it impossible to understand how they could suddenly be considered aliens, and interned as though they were Japs, or Jerries.

And, as at the Kelly farm, Mrs Firelli and her daughters, were in the same boat: trying to run an enormous market garden, on their own.

Annie, knowing full well that both Hannah and Dan had no time to spare, finished her tea, and made her way back home

***

As Annie was walking back to her house, Billy had been looking desolately out of the front window finding it extremely difficult to concentrate on Classical Greek. If Dr Scott doesn't come back, he reflected, miserably, then it wouldn't really matter if I learn Greek, or not; I'll never get to the matriculation exam now; that'd be the end of the scholarship.

From his window, he could see the shops and the small queue outside the baker's; his mind vaguely registered the fact that they must have some cakes at last, but he was not paying attention. His eyes then wandered to the fish shop and he saw, to his surprise, that the door was open!

He stared. Could Dr Scott have returned? Surely, he would have let me know? Perhaps I'm supposed to be over there studying, not here.

Billy leapt up from his seat, grabbed all the books he had on his desk and the papers he had been working on. He'd have plenty to show Dr Scott; he had finished all the work he had been given to do, and had learned by heart that whole new Latin passage from Cicero.

Dr Scott would be pleased with that!

Billy hurried from the house; then forced himself to slow down. Walk slowly, he ordered himself. If I hurry, I'll be breathless, unable to speak. Slow down … That's better. Arriving at the shops he smiled, and greeted the ladies, waiting in the queue, then entered the shop door.

"Dr Scott …" Billy began, then gave a strangled, piercing scream and fell across the threshold – books and papers flying everywhere.

The ladies in the queue rushed to him, and then looking into the room, began screaming hysterically themselves.

Dr Harold Scott was hanging from a beam in the roof, quite obviously and horribly dead!

CHAPTER 8

When Inspector Bob Peters and Sergeant Pierce arrived from Tavistock, they found a horribly familiar sight.

Annie Watson was seated on the ground, holding her son in her arms; he appeared to be unconscious while Annie was weeping uncontrollably. Mr Tanby had cut down the dead man and had laid him, reverently, on what had been the counter of the fish shop. An ambulance was waiting nearby and there were several army vehicles standing near the shop, with a number of military officers moving about.

Peters was relieved to see his old friend, Major Ted Waters, near Annie and the boy. He moved quickly to the army doctor.

"Major, what is the situation? How bad is Billy? What can we do?"

Dr Waters looked up. "Bob, I honestly don't know. He's had a terrible shock; he seems destined to have one fearful shock after another, the poor lad. I've sent for Kemp, he's Billy's doctor; he would know what's best to do."

"Is he still unconscious?"

"Yes, and I'm worried. It's been a long time now ..." Waters was interrupted by a wail of anguish from Annie.

"It's that terrible woman's fault! Arrest her, Inspector, she's a murderess just as surely as if she hung the poor man up herself."

Harriet McKenzie and Laura Hennessy crouching near Annie,

joined in the cries. "It's absolutely true!"; "That evil woman!"; "She's a wicked monster!"; "She's caused this!"

Inspector Peters looked at Pierce. "Mrs Watson – or, one of you ladies – please," he held up his hand, "please tell me: *who* is it you are talking about?" This produced a greater babble of noise from the ladies.

Peters turned to his colleague. "Sergeant," he ordered, "see if you can find out what that is all about; I'll see to the corpse; the army people are waiting for me."

***

An hour later, the inspector and sergeant were seated with Annie and Major Waters in Annie's kitchen.

Billy was in his own bed; Dr Kemp had given him a large injection, and at the moment, Billy was breathing normally. Annie's neighbour and good friend, Nan Brady, the dance pianist, had made a big pot of tea, and had insisted that Annie leave Billy's bedside and sit in her own kitchen. Nan had then taken Annie's place by the side of Billy.

"When you feel up to it, Mrs Watson," Inspector Peters said gently, "just tell me all you can about the dead man. They've taken him away back to the Military Hospital; he's their responsibility now, being a soldier."

Annie raised her stricken face. "Inspector, both Billy and I want to go to the funeral – it's the least we can do. Oh, I'm being ridiculous as usual! Billy will never be well enough in time. But Harry Scott was so young – to me, he was young – so his parents are most probably still living. I want to speak to them to tell them how wonderful their brave and good son was, and what he did for Billy!" She feared she would cry again, so turned her head away.

"We can certainly arrange that," Major Waters soothed Annie. "Now, Mrs Watson, the inspector must know about Lady Emily, and the connection with poor Dr Scott's death. Try and see if you can give him all the details."

The grey-haired Major grimaced. "I've told the inspector of the trouble we've had with her, and her 'bolshie' friend, at the Convalescent Hospital; that I've forbidden them to ever set foot in the place again, or I'll have them arrested by the guards."

Annie sat up. "I'm being a stupid, emotional nuisance as usual – you ought to be used to it by now, Inspector, and you too, Sergeant …"

"Nonsense, Mrs Watson," Sergeant Pierce broke in stoutly, "you've had a fearful shock. Just take your time." Annie blew her nose, firmly getting her thoughts in order.

"Well, the Lady Emily Gascoigne-Ridley is, as you would know, the aunt of the great doctor of the same name. She is a widow and is a pampered, useless, fool of a woman who was at a loose end. She suddenly decided to come here for the winter and to see what havoc she could wreak in our village. That sounds weird, but it's the absolute truth."

"You mean, Mrs Watson, this lady actually deliberately sets out to cause trouble?" Inspector Peters was confused. Annie Watson was the most charitable woman he had ever met, yet this sounded so unlike her. Perhaps it was just a clash of temperaments; a couple of relations who didn't get on? He had certainly had his share of what the police called, 'domestic' incidences.

"Exactly what I do mean, Inspector," Annie answered, "and look how she succeeds. She only arrived here Sunday and, by Sunday night, had broken the engagement of Penelope and young George McKenzie and the understanding between Joan Hennessy and Dan Kelly and then, look what she's done to Dr Scott."

"That's terrible, if that is what has happened. But how did Lady Emily bring about the death of Captain Scott? Was there any letter or anything? I asked the Army officers – also Mr Tanby – if they'd found a letter, and they said they hadn't. It's fairly usual to find a note of some sort, in a suicide."

As if in answer to the inspector's enquiry, there was a discreet knock on the back door of the kitchen. Sergeant Pierce was nearest, so opened the door. There was a hurried colloquy between the sergeant and Mr Tanby the butcher. Pierce came forward with a rather dirty envelope in his hands.

"Inspector, Mr Tanby has just found a letter addressed to Mrs Watson. He said it must have been pushed under his door early this morning, and must have slid under the sawdust.

"He only put down the new sawdust late last night, so it could only have been there since this morning. He said that customers had walked on the letter, not seeing it, and apologized for its condition."

Pierce handed the letter to his superior officer, who immediately handed it to Annie.

"You realise, Mrs Watson, that in a case of suicide, I'll have to see the letter, but I think you should read it first." Annie took the letter with hands that trembled, and carefully opened it. As she read it, again her eyes were tragic. When she had finished the short note, she handed it silently to Peters. He read it aloud:

"Mrs Watson. Please ask Billy to forgive me for what I'm about to do. If there were some alternative, please believe me, I would not leave him in the lurch like this. The truth of the matter is that some years ago, I did something stupid. I've regretted it ever since.

"Apparently, the Lady Emily found out about this. She came to see me in the fish shop. She told me, that if I did not cease, immediately, being Billy's tutor, she would make the whole sordid story public. I could not risk that for my parents' sake – it would break my mother's heart.

"Could I suggest another tutor for Billy? He is a truly gifted and brilliant boy and deserves to have an education. There is a Major Timothy Johnson at the Convalescent Hospital; he is a far better Classics scholar than I am and is a very good man, and one without any skeletons in his closet!

"Bless you and your family. You have been kindness itself to me.

I have treasured my time with your good son. Pray for me. Harold Scott."

Inspector Peters cleared his throat, while the Sergeant averted his eyes and stared blindly at the blank wall.

"Please forgive me, Mrs Watson," Peters said humbly, "I honestly thought you were exaggerating. I understand now you were simply stating the truth about this woman. I'm sorry, but I'll have to keep this letter." Annie nodded. Peters turned to the sergeant. "Come, Pierce, we'll go and make a call on her ladyship at the pub."

As they were leaving they were interrupted by the loud ringing of the phone. Annie automatically picked up the receiver. She recognized the doctor's wife, Thelma, but could hardly understand what she was saying. Annie motioned to Peters to wait.

"Please, Thelma, I beg of you, slow down; I can't understand you. Yes, Major Waters *is* here. Why? Good God! Where's Dr Kemp? … I understand. Yes, I'm sure Dr Waters will go immediately; he has a car … No, keep her there. Tell her the doctor is coming and he'll do everything possible for Dennis. I'll tell him now."

Annie faced the men. "Major Waters, the doctor's wife, Thelma Kemp, begs you to go immediately to the Nicholls' house – it's opposite the Kemps on the corner. Mr Nicholls has had a stroke; is unable to speak, and is paralysed down the entire left side of his body.

"Mrs Nicholls – who must be eighty, at least – ran to Thelma's. Dr Kemp is out on his house sick calls, and poor Edith Nicholls is in a bad way."

Annie looked at Inspector Peters intently. "If you want more confirmation of the intentions of the Lady Emily, let me tell you this: She went to see poor old Major Nicholls this morning, and asked to speak to him about his long army career, *especially stressing* his role in a campaign in the *Boer War*.

"Mrs Nicholls was unwilling to leave them, as her husband turned a vivid red, when the Boer War was mentioned, but he insisted on seeing Lady Emily alone.

"Poor Edith Nicholls found, to her horror, immediately after Lady Emily had left the house, her husband was in the state I've described. Mrs Nicholls is convinced it was Emily, who brought about the shock that caused the apoplexy."

Major Waters grabbed his bag and ran quickly to his car. Both Inspector Peters and Sergeant Pierce left shortly after. Annie, feeling drained and sick, went into Billy's room and put her arms around Nan Brady's shoulders.

"And now, Nan, it is poor old Mr Nicholls," she murmured.

"I heard you Annie. Dear God, is there no end to it all? If anything happens to Billy over this, I'll kill the wretched woman myself."

The idea that Nan Brady would actually say something like that made Annie smile, and she hugged the older woman. She whispered: "You and me both, Nan!" She looked at her son.

"Has he spoken, Nan?"

"Only once, Annie. He recognized me immediately – that's a good sign – and said: "Oh, Nan. Why?" started to cry, then was ashamed of his tears and buried his head in the pillow so I wouldn't see them. I think he's cried himself to sleep, which could be a good thing. The breathing's is still irregular, but it's better than it was; I've kept my fingers on the pulse."

"I think you're right. Nan, do you realise that, in the last year, Billy has withstood shocks that would kill a healthy person? Yet, the Specialists tell me that if he got a sudden shock, as small as a person suddenly sneezing, he could drop dead instantly. It's mystifying!"

Nan released her hold on Billy's hand, and took hold of Annie's. "Truly, Annie, only God knows why, we certainly don't." Nan warmed Annie's hands in her own, and stood up.

"I've got to go; I'm working tonight and have a heap of things to do beforehand. But, damn the work; if there's any change for the worst, call me instantly, and I'll come."

Annie hugged her neighbour. "You're the best friend I could ever have, Nan. No wonder Billy loves you." As Nan Brady left the house, Annie took her place at the bedside, and gently took her son's hand.

***

Major Timothy Johnson was talking to Betty Fletcher in the bar of the pub. There were only a couple of elderly men sitting quietly in the corner, making their drinks last as long as they could, for the room was warm and cosy, while outside a cold wind was blowing. Betty and Tim were grimly serious.

"She's killed the poor old bugger, that's what she's done, Betty."

"Certainly, in a moral sense she has, Tim, and the police can do nothing to her at all! It's all so rottenly unfair." Betty started to polish the bar which already was shining, in her agitation. "And, there's poor old Mrs Nicholls too …"

"How is she, have you heard?"

"Well, Thelma Kemp – that's the doctor's wife, she's a trained nursing sister – she rushed in to get some brandy. She said she didn't think Edith – Mrs Nicholls – will get over the shock – thinks it'll kill her."

"If Mr and Mrs Nicholls die as a result of this woman, she's scored three deaths in one day! It's beyond belief, Betty. Are the two of them in the house do you know?"

"Yes, they came in a little while ago. After Emily had been to the Nicholls, she went on the bus to Bexford while the other one – the bogus Russian – was at the Quarry area, but she's back now. Things obviously didn't go too well there, as Tanya Illich didn't stay away long.

"I thought she'd be there all day – she's got old Bert Liveridge on a string and no mistake. I had Mrs Liveridge in tears in the kitchen here."

"Betty, I've often meant to ask you. How many people actually work here; what exactly do you do? I know you wait in the bar, but it's only open at specific times. It's none of my business, but I was just curious."

Betty laughed. "The answer to the first part of the question is, that the number varies depending on whether we have guests or not, and how many of them. At the moment regarding the workers, we have Joe and Biddy – landlord and cook – and me. We're the permanent ones.

"Then we have the casuals: Mrs Liveridge helps in the kitchen, and also with the cleaning; Mrs Cookson, she does the great pile of washing and ironing; often we have another woman from the Quarry area as well, if we're extra busy, or there's a big function on.

"Then there's the outside work. Two elderly men work, as casuals, on the maintenance and general upkeep of the place – the lawns and gardens and such, and one of them is good with the barrels and cellar work. He's here most days; his name is Ben – a nice old bloke."

"And you, Betty?"

"Well, I do a bit of everything, Tim. Joe and Biddy Jones are getting on in years now and this place is very demanding; there's a lot of work to be done just to keep it going. So I've had to learn just about everything – help in the cooking, serving the meals, learning all about drinks, beer and cellar work, waiting in the bar – I even help with the cleaning when we're stuck.

"Then there's the office work; I help Jim with the bookwork. I do most of the accounts, and pay a lot of the bills – Jim put my signature on the cheque books, and with all the stupid and endless Government forms that we now have in wartime, I handle most of those as well. Quite frankly, Joe doesn't understand them. And why should he? He's an old man; he was eighty last birthday. I think he's incredible to be able to do what he does."

Betty laughed. "When you start listing the jobs, it sounds an awful lot, and I suppose it is; I'm just used to it and don't usually get fazed by it."

"Do you wait on the guests in their rooms?"

"Usually yes," Betty laughed. "But this time, I told her ladyship and her companion, that there was no room service, so if they wanted anything they would have to come down to the front desk, and ring the bell. They were furious!" Tim joined in the laughter.

Betty looked at the soldier closely. "And why, may I ask, do you want to know all about what I do?"

"Betty, you know damn well why I want to know all about you." Betty's cheeks flushed a rosy pink. 'I've been here three months now, and it's all about to end ..."

"Oh, no!" Betty exclaimed, before she could stop herself.

"Aha! That's the best thing I've heard all day! So you're sorry I'm leaving, are you?"

Betty struggled to retrieve this situation. "Well, of course. I would be sorry to see *any* soldier go back to war – any soldier, mind you – but, you see, I've got used to you, coming in of an afternoon and ..."

"And ..."

"Yes, damn you! I *will* miss you. Now, are you satisfied?"

"More than satisfied, Betty. I've wanted so much to speak to you, but I felt I had no right. You know my history. What if there's a relapse?"

"Why should there be? The doctors are delighted with you aren't they? So what if you've had a nervous breakdown? All those poor wretched soldiers down there at the Convalescent Hospital are in the same boat. Are we just to abandon them?"

"They have fought for our country and have been wounded; perhaps more terribly than if they'd received physical wounds. Those wounds can often heal easily and are usually over and done with, but the other sort of wounds ..."

"You're a wonderful girl, Betty, and highly intelligent and perceptive as well."

"Flattery will get you everywhere, but don't get carried away. I only went to school until I was nearly fifteen. I would have loved to be able to stay at school – I loved learning, especially History, but with Dad dead, and Mum working as a cook, I had to start work." She smiled. "I'm pretty dumb actually. About the only thing I know how to do is run a pub."

"And, what's wrong with that? And don't belittle yourself, Betty. To run a successful business is not for dummies."

"All right, then, *Major* Johnson," Betty assumed an interrogative manner. "What about your background? I know nothing about you at all. Really, you could be Jack the Ripper and I wouldn't know it."

"Well, if I am, you don't think I'm going to admit it," Tim laughed. "No, Betty, my background is pretty boring. I was fortunate enough to be born into a family fairly well off, and so was sent to good schools, then on to University.

"I taught for a while at Uni, but Dad wanted me to join him in the business, so I only kept up my studies, as a hobby. I would have liked to have been able to stay at the University teaching."

"Oh, I do envy you that, Tim – your education, I mean. I think I do understand the attraction of Socialism, indeed Communism, when they go on about the poor never getting a chance to climb the ladder of education."

"It's true that University education is mainly restricted to those who can pay the enormous fees, Betty, but there *are* other ways."

"Scholarships, you mean? The problem with those, Tim, is that you have to be able to *stay* at school those extra years, to be eligible, to sit for the examinations. There's night-school, of course. That's one way to try for a scholarship; I know a number of ambitious young people try that."

"Well, that's what poor Harry Scott did. He was truly brilliant and his parents were very poor. He won a University Scholarship and then, while at Uni, worked at night to keep alive, yet still did brilliantly in his examinations. He was a pretty inspiring bloke, actually. That's what makes it all so bloody dreadful."

Betty began to be alarmed, seeing Tim so upset – this was

dangerous for him. She was glad of a sudden distraction occurring in the hall. Excusing herself, Betty went out to the hall and welcomed Inspector Peters and Sergeant Pierce.

"A terrible business, Betty," Peters shook hands. "Is Lady Emily here at the moment?"

"It is, Inspector, and yes, her pestilential ladyship is in residence!"

"Before you let her know I'm here, Betty, tell me, have you heard anything more about Mr Nicholls, or his wife?"

"Only rumours, Inspector. I think Mr Nicholls is in a very bad way. He's been taken away by ambulance; he's not expected to live – Major Waters arranged the ambulance. And Mrs Nicholls is still at Thelma Kemp's house – I don't know the latest on the old lady. They've waiting for Dr Kemp to return from his house-calls. They've managed to contact him – a neighbour took a message to him."

"Oh well, we might get some news later. I was hoping to have it before I saw the Lady Emily, and her companion – later will have to do. Would you lead us up to her, please Betty."

Betty moved to the stairs and Peters and Pierce saw Tim Johnson at the bar. They waved to each other then followed Betty up the wide staircase.

Back at the bar, Tim sat thinking of a plan. Divide and conquer! I wonder if that would work. I'll give it a try anyhow, the first chance I get. I've read plenty of 'bolshie' material in my time at Uni, so that'd be a piece of cake. Yes, divide and conquer! Sometimes, the old ways are the best – more effective anyhow!

CHAPTER 9

Without knocking, Betty threw open the door of the sitting room, catching the two occupants by surprise. Lady Emily was moving towards the table where Tanya was seated, writing notes.

Lady Emily made a great deal of wide-open eyes, fluttering lashes, and agitated movements with her soft little pampered hands, but Peters saw that it was the woman, with the Russian name, who actually was the one, who was truly alarmed.

Tanya's hand, in her agitation, had grabbed at the thin gold chain around her neck, with such force, that the Inspector thought it must surely break. He noted that her eyes were wide with fear, but she was the first to recover.

Standing up, Tanya addressed Betty in frigid tones, her 'Russian' accent perfectly in place.

"Miss Fletcher, in decent places, it is thought customary to knock on the door, before entering it with strangers." Betty was not the slightest perturbed.

"How would you know, Ethel? You've never before lived in 'decent' places; this is the closest you've ever come to knowing what such places are like."

Tanya actually hissed with fury. "You will be sorry for that, Miss Fletcher! I would advise you to call me by my *legal* name. It is Miss Tanya Illich."

"Oh, that's right, Ethel. Reading some Russian novels, were you?

That's a surprise; I didn't know you could read."

"Betty …" warned Peters. She smiled pertly at him, and spoke loudly: "Inspector Peters and Sergeant Pierce, may I present you to Comrade Emily – alias Lady Emily Gascoigne-Ridley – and her accomplice, Miss Tanya Illich – alias Ethel Sparks. They're here in Bexford North to convert all of us to the Soviet cause; to urge our soldiers to desert, to denounce the war, and to help bring about the great purge, so that the streets will flow with blood."

Betty caught the look again in Peters' eye and hastily removed herself from the room.

There was complete silence in the room after Betty had left. Inspector Peters motioned Lady Emily to sit down and he and Pierce sat down, uninvited, at the table. He looked fixedly at Lady Emily, who continued her pantomime of distress.

Peters suddenly realised that she was enjoying herself immensely; she was the centre of attention, and was revelling in it. Peters deliberately turned his chair, so that he was looking at Tanya, and directed all his questions to her.

"I want an account of your day's activities up to this minute, Miss Illich, and I want them quickly."

"Why should you address yourself to me in this manner? What have I done that is against the law?"

"That remains to be seen …"

"I can tell you, all you …" began Lady Emily.

Without looking at her, Peters said to Tanya. "I don't need to know about Lady Emily; her activities are known to the whole village – she is utterly, and completely unimportant."

"How dare …"

"Miss Illich, I am still waiting …"

"Well, this morning, I went on foot to the Quarry area …"

"Whom did you see there?"

"Firstly, I called in at the dairy, but they were busy, so then went on to Bert Liveridge's house in Quarry Lane."

"How long were you there?"

"Not long; there was an unfortunate misunderstanding …"

"About what?"

"Some pamphlets I had given Bert to study …"

"Confiscate those pamphlets, Pierce …" Tanya began hurriedly picking up an assortment of pamphlets, while Sergeant Pierce loomed over her. She was frightened and confused. Why was *she* being questioned? It was Emily they wanted – Emily who had caused all this unnecessary trouble.

Peters continued his severe interrogation.

"You mentioned a misunderstanding. Tell me who was involved in that?"

"Well, it was really nothing …"

"Every time you begin a sentence with, 'well', I know you're lying. Tell me about the misunderstanding."

"Well … I mean … It was between Mrs Liveridge and her husband; she didn't want him reading my pamphlets; I was trying to explain them to her."

"Were other people involved?"

"Some people from the other houses – who had sons overseas – they were a little upset and …"

"Because they were told that their sons were dying and being tortured in vain; that the war was all wrong …" Peters finished the sentence.

Tanya's temper flared: "Well, I believe it is! And I don't care how many times I use the word 'well'; I *am* not lying. And, what's wrong with what I am doing? There's no law against it, is there?"

"In actual fact there is, Miss Illich. You could be tried for treason in time of war; I'll have to get advice on the matter. As for your companion! Do you enjoy being in the company, *and being in the employ*, of a woman, who drives good people to their deaths by blackmail?"

Tanya gasped. She shot a quick look at Lady Emily. Peters continued to look only at her. The young woman raged, mentally: Why won't he address *Emily*? She's the one who apparently has done all the damage.

"I'm waiting, Miss Illich …"

"But I don't know how to answer. What has Lady Emily done that is so dreadful?"

"She has deliberately, and with malice aforethought, brought about the death of a fine young wounded soldier, then, not content with that, she caused poor old Mr Nicholls, who must be eighty-five if he's a day, to have a stroke; he is paralysed and dying, and his wife is likely to die as well."

"I didn't know," Tanya gasped again, "at least – about the old people …"

"Aha! So you *did* know about the young soldier. That makes you an accomplice."

"No, no, I only knew Lady Emily said that it was not right for her relative to be coached by a man, with a criminal record … that's all I know."

Inspector Peters actually believed her. Tanya Illich might be everything he detested, but by her own lights, she was an honest woman. He kept his face like granite, as he rose from his chair.

"I would advise you both to make sure you remain at this hotel, until we have finished with you; neither of you is permitted to leave. I would like never to have to be in the same polluted room with either of you again, but needs must.

"As a matter of fact, you both disgust me." Peters picked up his hat. "I shall be in touch with you later."

The two men closed the door behind them, leaving a deadly silence in the room. Tanya was mentally considering her patroness, while maintaining a blank facial expression.

If what that policeman said was true, and she had to admit she thought it was, then, perhaps Emily has served her purpose; she could now be too dangerous to the Cause – perhaps too dangerous to let live very much longer.

An accident, perhaps? She could easily blame it on one of the people she has harmed. But…This needed more thinking on – she'd have to be very careful.

***

Ten minutes later, Lady Emily heard children's voices calling her name, outside the window. She had been roused to a seething fury by Inspector Peters' treatment of her; she needed something desperately now to restore her feelings of superiority, to their usual level.

She quickly rose from her chair, went to the window, opened it wide and stood framed in the opening. She was pleased to see a group of children standing below, looking up.

Emily smiled condescendingly at the children and was gratified to hear a cry of exultation go up when they caught sight of her. Another shout went up, when Tanya – far more conversant with the ways of small children, than the Lady Emily – hurried to stand beside her.

"Listen, Tanya, isn't that sweet," cooed Lady Emily.

"Ssh! Listen to what they're saying." The two women stood silently and listened intently. The children's sweet voices carried clearly in the still air:

"Lady Emily Gascoigne-Ridley
Drinks like a fish and is often tiddly;
With a name like that, she is, you see,
Thoroughly wicked, and so she be."

Lady Emily was outraged; she opened her mouth to speak, when an egg hit her squarely on the forehead and dripped down her face. Her mouth remained open in shock. Tanya, her worst fears confirmed, was just about to slam the window shut, when another egg hit her on the bridge of the nose, with disastrous results. Both women were streaming with egg.

Without a word being spoken, they rushed from the room and ran down the stairs, where the first person they encountered was Betty, who was dusting the hall.

Betty took one look and realised what had happened. She had heard the children singing and had been chuckling to herself. She stood in front of the two women; her arms on her hips.

"Now, now, this won't do, I'm sorry, but it just won't. You'll just have to make do with porridge and toast tomorrow morning. I see you've already had your egg ration. Don't waste any; you might be able to scape a little from your chin, or your dresses.

"Anyhow, no eggs tomorrow for either of you, remember that." Betty went on with her dusting, whistling tunefully.

Lady Emily fled back upstairs in a rage. Tanya was cut from a different cloth. She stared at Betty, then very slowly, went out the back door of the pub, to the tap in the yard. She washed her face and neck, and drenching her handkerchief in water, mopped up the mess on her blouse and skirt.

"When she had cleaned herself, but was clearly very wet, she marched into the bar, rang the bell and demanded of Betty, a large gin and tonic. Betty raised her eyebrows, served Tanya in silence, and then watched this strange, young woman go to an alcove near the window from which she could see the street.

Major Tim Johnson was still sitting near the bar, so winking at Betty, he seized his chance, and went with his drink, to Tanya.

Tim paused near the table Tanya was using. He coughed apologetically. Tanya looked up at his handsome, embarrassed face.

"I say, do you mind if I join you? I've been longing to talk with you and couldn't summons up the … er … guts." Tanya smiled; it was not often handsome young men, asked if they could sit with her.

"If you want to, do so – the chairs belong to all …"

"That's awfully kind of you," Tim sat down. "By the way, my

name's Tim, Tim Johnson but I'd be happy, if you'd call me Tim. You see I've read a lot of your literature, and I think you've shown me the way. I've been searching for some direction in my life, for the past three years – ever since I've been in the army." Tanya looked with greater interest at this diffident young man.

"I'm delighted to hear you say so. My name's Tanya Illich, but please call me Tanya."

"May I? Golly, that's great. Miss … sorry, Tanya. I am truly mixed up about this war. You see I volunteered right at the beginning, but after seeing what I've seen, especially in Germany, I don't know anymore, whether it was right or not."

"You are right to wonder. Have you read my pamphlet: 'If you're a Patriot, Refuse to Fight'? If you are genuine, you could find that helpful."

"Yes, it was that one that really got me thinking. You see, Tanya, after three years of fighting in terrible places and seeing frightful things I became ill – not physically, but mentally," he lowered his voice, "you won't tell anyone will you?"

Tanya was touched. Here, before her, was an example of exactly what she had been saying, and writing. The poor men were not to blame; it was their blasted superiors, who were, in turn, taking orders from their imperial masters – the Upper Classes. Tanya did an unexpected thing; she took Tim's hand in hers, and pressed it sympathetically.

"Oh course, I won't tell," she promised. "It will remain a secret with me. But let's get this whole subject clear …"

"Excuse me for interrupting, Tanya, but I'm troubled about Russia's role in this war – that's what's holding me back."

"Oh?"

"You see, Russia signed a non-aggression pact with Hitler at the beginning of the war, and yet, now, she has joined the Allies – in spite of the pact. It didn't seem right to me; I was disappointed with Stalin doing that – going back on his word, I mean."

"I can understand your difficulty in accepting that, Tim, but it actually was a very clever thing for Russia to do."

"Was it?"

"Well, we both know that Germany with its Empire is now finished; it'll only be a fairly short time now until Europe is in total ruins.

"It was now the *opportune time*, for Russia to enter the war – with its magnificent army – to come to the rescue of the effete West. They will now be seen as the saviours of the Allies, who are exhausted."

"I see."

"But," continued Tanya, "as soon as the war in Europe is over, then there will be *three* major powers: England, America, *and Russia*. Europe will have to be divided into *three* sections, and Russia will get *one third* of the whole of Europe.

"It will then be able to impose Communist rule, on millions of people and bring about the freedom of the working classes."

"I see, yes, jolly clever," observed Tim slowly. "I'm sorry, Tanya, but it still sounds a bit underhand to me – posing as a friend, just to get what you want …"

"Oh, Tim, I think you have been brought up to believe in Absolutes, haven't you?"

"Absolutes?" Tim sounded as if he were genuinely puzzled.

"You know, belief in 'God' as an absolute; 'Truth' as an absolute – you know what I mean; you must have studied *some* philosophy – you are an educated man."

"Oh dear, I now understand what you mean. Yes, I'm afraid you're right; I have been brought up that way, Tanya; the family are strong church-goers." Tim managed to sound apologetic.

"That's always a problem, Tim, to get over. But once you discover that there are *no* Absolutes you are free to use Truth in any way you like, as long as it ultimately leads to the victory of the proletariat. Let me explain …"

For the next fifteen minutes Tim listened to this woman,

realising, for the first time, that she was utterly sincere, and believed in the gospel of Marx, as fervently as the most ardent evangelist. She had convincing arguments as well.

Tim realised how extremely pernicious this doctrine was to be preaching in wartime, and also how *alluring* it was, in its black and white simplicity. He shook himself mentally, and hastened to put his plan into action.

"Yes, Tanya, that is extremely well put. I do so agree with you," he shuffled a bit in his chair. "Would you think it an awful cheek if I offered you some advice?"

Tanya was surprised. "No, of course not."

"Well, it's about your travelling companion, the Lady Emily …" he seemed reluctant to go on.

"Well, what about her?"

"It's difficult to say this, but do you think it's helpful to your Cause to have her with you? You see, here in the village, I have nothing to do and I have heard all the gossip about you and the lady. On the whole, the people are not objecting to *you*, but they positively hate the Lady Emily."

"Really? Are you sure of that, Tim?"

"Most definitely. You see, Tanya, she keeps interfering in people's lives, and causing mischief, which sets people against *you*, and that's not fair, in my opinion."

"No, it isn't. Yes, she *does* interfere; why, I don't know … she has everything anyone could want but is still dissatisfied. I can't understand it."

"And," continued Tim, "now with these deaths – especially the young soldier, Harry Scott …"

"What exactly *did* she do, Tim? The inspector was so horrible – terrifying really – that all I gathered was that the soldier was dead, but how did that involve Lady Emily?"

"You really don't know?"

"No, truly I don't. Was it bad?"

Tim explained Lady Emily's role in the death of Captain Scott and the letter that had been left by the dead man. Tanya was shaken.

"And he actually hanged himself on account of what Lady Emily threatened?"

"Yes, Tanya, he did."

"That's a dreadful thing to do; he was a wounded man as well. Simply dreadful!" Tanya stared into space for a moment.

"Tim, thank you for telling me about this; I'll not forget it." She stood up. "Please excuse me, but I want to go to my room; there's something I've got to sort out in my mind. Something I have to do, and I'm not sure just how to do it."

Tim stood up as Tanya left the table. He was actually impressed with the woman. She is, he believed, utterly and completely sincere and, he thought, as honest a woman as she is incredibly dangerous.

In the solitude of her bedroom, Tanya pondered on all that the soldier Tim had told her. Lady Emily was certainly useful in terms of material assistance, but if she was detrimental to the Cause, then she would have to go. Tanya's fingers absently played with the buttons on her cardigan as she pondered her next move.

***

Later that evening, after a meal eaten mainly in silence, Tanya and Lady Emily were seated in their sitting room. They had carried their own coffee upstairs with them.

Tanya was trying to think of a topic of conversation, when Lady Emily, who had been making several attempts of her own to speak, actually forestalled Tanya. Her tone was serious.

"Tanya, I have to speak to you about a very serious matter."

"Yes, my Lady."

"You may not have realised it, but I'm not liked in this village."

Tanya tried hard to keep a straight face. How could this idiot of a woman have imagined otherwise? She raised her eyebrows in simulated amazement.

"Really? Surely, that isn't so."

"Yes, it is, Tanya. I think it's entirely possible that someone will try to kill me."

"Oh really, Lady Emily, that's plain ridiculous!" Tanya smiled. "This is Australia, not the wild west."

"No, dear, I truly am serious about this," she held up her small hands. "Please dear, don't say any more about it. I *know* I'm right; that's why I went to a solicitor today in Bexford. I've made a new Will."

Good gracious, thought Tanya, this stupid woman *is* actually serious!

"A Will?"

"Yes, dear, and please don't be offended, but I've cut out all my relations and I've left everything to you – every single thing."

Tanya nearly fainted. "You *what*?" she gasped.

"Yes, everything goes to you at my death: the town houses at Vaucluse and Double Bay, the beach house at Palm Beach, the bonds and shares, the jewellery and all the cash.

"You will realise, dear, that I'm not exactly sure how much the total amount is.

"I asked my solicitor just how much it would be, in general terms; he said about half a million pounds. You realise, dear, that I could be out a £100,000 or so."

"Oh, a mere 100,000 thousand pounds, or so," Tanya gasped weakly – she needed a stiff drink; she thought she might easily swoon in a minute … or wake up … This couldn't be really happening! This kind of thing only happens on the Pictures!

While Tanya's mind was trying to cope with this shock, the de-testable upper-class, voice went on:

"So, that's all dear, really. I just wanted you to know, that being with you has given me a sense of purpose I've never had before in my life and you have been a perfect travelling companion.

"And, most importantly of all, Tanya: making this Will today, means that, if and when, something happens to me, you'll be secure for the rest of your life."

Lady Emily stood up, kissed Tanya lightly on the forehead – a most unusual gesture for her – and moved to the door. She moved slowly as if she were unwell.

"Please excuse me Tanya. I don't feel well; I think I'll make it an early night. Good night dear."

Tanya was vaguely aware of the reply she made, but was holding tightly to the table; her head was reeling. She forced herself to realise that what she had heard was *reality* – not fantasy! She was awake, not dreaming!

This was the most astonishing thing that had ever happened to her in her whole life. She would be one of the richest women in Australia! But, far more important than that: she would have the funds necessary to further the Revolution, in a way that none of her fellow travellers could even dream of, in their wildest dreams.

She crept out of the room, pushed the old door of their room as quietly as she could – it was slightly warped by age and tended to stick – went down the stairs to the bar, and ordered a double whisky.

Taking the whisky back up to the room, Tanya sipped it slowly, and as the colour started to return to her face with the drink – without the slightest twinge of conscious – she began to plan Lady Emily's sudden death, so that it would appear to be caused by someone else – someone here in the village.

CHAPTER 10

A cold mist swept through the village on Thursday morning, reminding the people that winter was underway. Cardigans and jumpers were dug out of storage, while Wellington boots were carefully checked for spiders which had made their homes in them, during the summer.

At the pub, the warmest room was the bar, with its big, log fire. After breakfast, Lady Emily informed Tanya that she would be spending the day in the bar, sitting near the window; she was feeling fragile, as well as cold.

She said she expected to see some of the villagers during the morning; she had the feeling that some of them might pop in to see her on local matters, they needed to discuss.

This didn't make any sense at all to Tanya. Why on earth would the people want to come to see the woman they hated? And, to discuss *local* issues? Why *should* they for goodness sake; Emily was not a local!

Tanya mentally shrugged; what did it really matter? It satisfied the ego of the stupid woman and it left her free to go where she wanted on her own.

What Emily didn't tell Tanya, was that she had rung a number of village people, telling – virtually *ordering* – them, to come to see her, in the pub. She had told them she had vital, secret, information to tell them, seriously concerning their families. She had even stipulated the time they were to come.

As Tanya set off on her own, Emily settled herself comfortably in the window seat and, seeing both Betty and the landlord in the same room, took the opportunity of complaining to both that her bed had been freezing.

She was informed sharply by Betty, if she wanted a hot-water bottle, she would have to bring hers down to the kitchen and fill it herself from the boiler each night, before bed.

Emily then complained – to a totally, indifferent Betty – about the delicate condition of her stomach, then ordered a bottle of soda water. Betty, with a look of utter contempt, took the bottle, with a glass, to the lady's table, and left the bar.

***

At nine o'clock, the news spread through the village that both the elderly couple, Mr and Mrs Nicholls had died.

Dennis Nicholls had not recovered from the stroke and had died during the night. Edith, his wife, sitting by the bedside of her husband of sixty years in the hospital, heard him struggling to say her name, as he was dying and, in her grief, had a massive heart attack and died by his side.

The village was shocked; the Nicholls had been there as long as anyone could remember and as there were no children of the marriage, there was a rent in the seam of village life which no one could repair.

Amelia Tatley was the first to bring the news to Annie whose genuine distress, equalled that of the elderly spinster's.

They had both loved the dear old couple. Annie remembered, with acute anguish, Edith Nicholls' previous enthusiastic participation – despite her great age – in the ladies' occupational therapy group, at the Convalescent Hospital.

Annie could still see Edith in her mind, dancing with the young soldiers Annie was teaching – all as young as Edith's great nephews – singing along with all of them happily, as they danced.

"Truly, Annie," Amelia murmured brokenly, "they were so well until yesterday, until the visit from that woman. What on earth could she have had against an inoffensive old couple like the Nicholls?"

"God alone knows, Amelia. You have to be some kind of monster to derive pleasure from the sufferings of others. I think – from Billy's books – that the term, now for that, is 'masochist'; yes, that's it – it's called 'masochism'.

"But I've had enough; not only do I have to share the shame of acknowledging that the Lady Emily is my relation, but she has been instrumental in nearly killing my boy, besides ruining any chance he has of going to University.

Annie's mobile face showed contempt. "Did you know, Amelia, she phoned me and asked me to 'attend' on her this morning; *attend* on her – who the dickens does she think she is? Has she become royal overnight?

"However, I'll go when I feel like going; she's not going to dictate to me when I come or go."

Amelia reached forward and held Annie's hand. "She's sent for me, too, Annie. That's what decided me!"

"I beg your pardon, Amelia? I don't understand."

"She's sent a note for me. I'm going to tackle her myself. She's going to hear from me exactly what I think of her." Annie was alarmed. Amelia was elderly; she was no match for Emily.

"Please think carefully of what you are doing, Amelia. She's a very clever and dangerous woman."

"No, Annie, I must. I've thought about it, and prayed about it; I know it's my duty." Once Amelia had said that, Annie knew there was no stopping her now that she considered it her duty.

"Perhaps I should have gone myself earlier, Amelia. Anyway, I'll go and see what she wants when I can get away; perhaps tomorrow.

She'll get an earful I can tell you." The two friends smiled grimly and then Amelia went in to sit by Billy's bed.

***

"I'm sorry, Edward, but I feel strongly about this, and as she has sent for me, I'm going," Thelma Kemp put down the teapot with unnecessary force. "She can't be allowed to get away with it."

"The police interviewed her yesterday, dear," Dr Kemp pointed out. "I don't think she's done anything that the law can touch. She's just a mischief-making woman."

"Well, she's going to hear what I think of her behaviour. Coming here, pumping us dry like gormless yokels, for all the confidences we had, then using them to destroy people's lives. She's an evil woman."

"I agree with you there, love. But, if you do go to her, be careful won't you? She's a tricky woman."

"Oh, I'll be careful, Edward dear. I assure you, no one will see me putting cyanide in her drink." Husband and wife laughed; Edward began putting on a thick, warm, overcoat, as he went out to begin his rounds.

***

"Major Johnson, in the letter left by Captain Scott, he mentioned your name," informed Major Ted Waters. He was sitting in his office, at the Convalescent Hospital, with the soldier-patient, Tim Johnson, with whom he had become friendly.

"Did he? I knew him well, you know. He was a brilliant teacher and had a wonderful brain. I always thought he should have been in army intelligence, rather than the infantry, but that's army isn't it?"

"Too right, Tim," laughed Ted Waters, "if you say you were a cook you end up as a commando, and if you were a gym instructor, you end up as a cook. Anyhow, Tim, poor Harry suggested that you might take over the tutoring of young Billy Watson, for the matriculation exam. Would you be prepared to do that?"

"Of course, I would, Ted, but how can I? I'll be finished here in a couple of weeks, and sent – God knows where – somewhere in the Pacific, I would think."

"That of course is possible, but if there were a senior man, at your level, needed at either the hospital here, or up at the huge Military General Hospital – it would be only administration, I'm sorry to say – but would you be interested?"

"I have been in the war for more than three years now and this is the first break I've actually had. I can't say I'm relishing going back to the blood, mud and slush of the front line, but equally, I don't want any favours done for me.

"I enrolled to serve my country, and however corny that sounds, I meant exactly what I said: I have no intention of becoming a chocolate soldier."

"The truth of the matter is, Tim," admitted Ted, seriously, "that I'm worried about you returning to the front. Dr Gascoigne-Ridley – who's the best in this field, as you know – said that, in his opinion, you could be in trouble, if you face it again." Tim Johnson's face clouded and saddened.

"So he actually thinks I'll go looney again, Ted? Is that it? Don't be afraid to tell me the truth. It's important I know, especially now."

"Not 'looney' Tim, *never* say that. You are a sensitive, intelligent man who was faced with great horrors; you handled them magnificently, but it became a trauma that your whole nervous system couldn't cope with – that's all.

"Tim, that's not 'looney'! And, I *personally* don't want you to be exposed to it again, if I can help it.

"If that's getting preferential treatment, then I don't care: three years of where you've been, is miles more than others, have done. If you're positioned in Australia in the army, you're still serving your country."

"Well, Ted," Tim Johnson stood up, "let's just leave it to the authorities. If they decide to leave me here, well and good and I'll most definitely tutor Billy; if they decide I'm needed elsewhere, then that's it, as far as I'm concerned. O K?"

"All right, Tim, I'll let you know the moment I hear anything." Major Waters also stood up. "What are you going to do today? See Betty, I hope," he smiled. "I think she's a wonderful girl." Major Tim Johnson actually blushed.

"Actually, I intend to have a word to Lady Emily first – she rang to say she wanted to see me; I don't know why. However, I intend to tell her, I consider her a murderer. Harry Scott was a good friend of mine and a fine human being. I'm off to the pub soon." The two friends shook hands, and Tim left the office.

***

Mrs Hennessy sat at the breakfast table with her daughter Joan.

"Won't you at least consider, Joan, talking to Lady Emily about Dan? I cannot believe that he has done anything wrong and I think you're being foolish in being so ready to believe badly of him."

"So, it's all my fault, is it?"

Laura Hennessy sighed. "Don't talk about 'faults', Joan. Believe me, if you break off this engagement to Dan, you could well be truly sorry; he's a good lad, a hard worker, a wonderful son to his good hard-working mother …"

"Oh, for Heaven's sake! If he's so wonderful, marry him yourself," snapped Joan, a pretty girl, dressed in her VAD uniform. "Anyway we weren't officially engaged; we just had an understanding," she stood up.

"I'm off to the hospital – there are *real* men there; I'm *not* going to speak to the Lady Emily. You can if you like; I don't really care!"

"As a matter of fact I *am* going to speak to her; she sent a message for me to see her this morning, why, I cannot guess." Laura Hennessy found she was talking to thin air; Joan had grabbed her coat, her bag, as soon as her mother had begun to speak, and had run for the bus.

Laura Hennessy sat still at the table, her tea getting cold. All right, I *will go*! I didn't intend to do so, but I will go, and tell that … that – she looked around guiltily even though she was alone in the house – that *bitch* – exactly what I think of her.

She's as good as murdered three people, broken two engagements, and only God knows, if she's killed young Billy, into the bargain. Yes, I damn well will deal with the mischief-making, Lady Emily. I'll go to the pub. Now!

***

Dan Kelly was talking to his good friend and neighbour, Bianca Firelli.

"Well, I think it's pretty damn peculiar, but she's asked to see me. Whatever for, I can't think – I've never even met her.

"I'm going down to the pub to see the 'wicked witch' from the wild-wood now, Bianca. I've had enough of her, and her rotten insinuations. Joan has broken off with me and I've heard that Penny Watson and George McKenzie have broken up also."

The beautiful Italian girl stood as tall as Dan; her heavy load of black hair, carelessly tied back with a piece of string and her work clothes of trousers and shirt, actually adding to her true beauty.

"And you know, Dan, don't you, of her involvement in that poor soldier's suicide?"

"It's bloody shameful, and no one seems to be doing anything about it. I did hear that Inspector Peters saw her yesterday …"

"A lot of use that would be …"

"No… be fair, Bianca. You know Bob Peters is a decent bloke; he's totally opposed to your dad and brothers' internment. I think it's bloody rotten, myself."

Bianca looked thoughtfully at her neighbour. "You're a good man, Dan Kelly. Joan Hennessy is a fool."

Dan looked up startled. He had never, seriously, considered Bianca as … a *girl*, before; both of them worked like navvies on their farms. He was suddenly aware, that she was a very desirable woman, no longer a girl… Had he been stupidly blind all these years?

He was suddenly confused and embarrassed. He actually blushed and began to stutter.

"Bianca, I'm going to tell that revolting woman off. Do … you want …I mean would you …like … to come? … you don't have to … I mean … you could wait outside in the sulky … or … if the bar's open … I…I could buy you … a drink?"

Bianca giggled. "It's just as well that Dad and my brothers, *are* interned, Dan. Such a suggestion to a good Italian girl, is tantamount to a proposal of marriage.

"But, we're in Australia, and I'm an Australian, so I'll come to the pub for a drink with you and be glad to do so. I'll have to go just as I am, in working clothes; I've got a mountain of work piled up for me when I get back."

Laughing together and, for the first time in their entire lives, a little shy with each other, they climbed into the sulky and set off for the pub.

***

Stephen Armitage was talking to his old friend Constable Potts. They were walking around the garden.

"It's looking great Captain," the elderly Constable exclaimed, "even in its winter dress."

"It's mainly due to you, old fellow," Stephen laughed. "All the work you've done here with me, during the past three months! Well, it's turned out pretty well."

"I've loved every minute of it, truly I have." The two old friends sat on a garden seat. "I can't stay long, Captain, the inspector will pick me up on his way back from the Military Hospital. I just wanted to tell you I was so happy to hear the news – about you becoming a father! Truly, it's a miracle, that's what it is!"

Stephen put his arm around the shoulders of the elderly man. "You're a good sort, Potsy. And if, please God, it all goes well, both Florence and I want you to be the Godfather; there's absolutely no one else we'd prefer."

Constable Potts had to have recourse to his handkerchief, to blow his nose, vigorously, and cleared his throat several times. As usual, he covered his emotion, with a little joke.

"It would depend, of course, on who the Godmother was to be. She'd have to be extra special."

"Would Annie Watson fit the bill, by any chance?"

Potts clapped his hands. "The very name I was hoping you'd say." He shook hands solemnly with Stephen. "Captain Armitage, this is the greatest honour you could ever give me. I accept with gratitude." He stood up.

"Now, I'll have to be going; Inspector Peters is one of the finest superior officers I've ever served under, and I don't want to keep him waiting; I'll wait outside."

"I'll come with you, Potsy. I'm going to the pub to speak to that vicious and evil woman, the Lady Emily.

"Do you know she had the nerve to phone, and actually *told* me, to be at the pub at a certain time? Talk about *arrogance*! However, she'll get no polite words from me, the bitch.

"Apart from all the tragedy she caused other families, when Florence heard about the soldier and Billy, she fainted. Dr Kemp was frantic with worry, for the child.

"Thanks be to God, it seems as if all is well. Potts, I'll poison that vicious Emily if she has killed my child."

Potts was agitated by Stephen's words. "Don't say that, please Stephen, please don't ever say that!" He looked up.

"Here's the inspector. Say goodbye to your lovely wife, Captain; I'll see you before you go back to war, I promise."

Stephen waved to the inspector and made his way to the pub. He noted that, after Potts had entered the car, Inspector Peters took a pile of papers from his case, and was explaining them to the elderly constable. The police car remained parked near the Armitage gate.

***

Captain Stephen Armitage found Betty at the bar so bought a drink, swallowed it quickly and asked Betty where her ladyship was. He then followed Betty's pointed finger to an alcove near the window. Betty smiled at Stephen, then went to collect glasses from the kitchen.

The window seat was partially obscured from the bar by some fancy screens, and tall potted palms. Stephen was dimly aware of a figure sitting with her back to him, as he wended his way through other tables and chairs to the alcove.

The woman did not turn round at his approach. On the table, was a near-empty drinking glass.

Stephen looked at the still figure and his heart suddenly lurched sickeningly. He gently touched the shoulder, and the body fell, face sideways facing him onto the table, sending the glass crashing to the floor.

He stared in astonishment and horror. He forced himself to bend down and sniff the open mouth. There was a distinct, but faint, smell of almonds.

The lady was dead! Poisoned by cyanide! Oh my God! She's been murdered!

Stephen forced himself to look again at the face; *this* time his brain actually registered the *identity of the person* he was seeing!

He felt his senses reeling and grabbed, frantically, at a chair to prevent himself from falling.

The dead woman was *not* Lady Emily. It was *TANYA ILLICH!*

CHAPTER 11

Stephen Armitage struggled to stand upright then tried, desperately, to think clearly. The police! Yes, he *must* get the police. An image flashed into his mind: the two policemen sitting talking in the car at his front gate.

If he ran quickly he might be able to catch them – before they returned to Tavistock; that would save time.

Stephen turned and ran to the door, pausing just in time, to prevent Betty losing control of a large tray of newly washed glasses she was bringing from the kitchen, for the bar.

"Whoa there, Captain Armitage!" she cried, as she rescued the tray and put it down on the bar. "You nearly had me over! What's the hurry?" Betty smiled again at the man, then for the first time noticed his white face and agitation. "What is it? What has happened?"

"Betty," Stephen gasped, "I'm going to get the police; I might be able to catch them."

"Why, what's happened?"

"Betty, the woman's dead; she's been murdered!"

"Whaaaat?" Betty staggered in her shock.

"Yes, murdered. Betty … don't let anyone go near the woman – it's now a crime scene. I'll be back as quickly as I can."

Stephen ran through the hall and into the street. From the hotel steps he could see the police car still standing at his gate. He increased his speed; hoping he might get there in time.

***

Betty Fletcher stood holding the bar until her head cleared. Merciful God what's going to happen now, she wondered? Not that anyone liked Lady Emily, but to have her *murdered*!

Yes, she decided, I must notify her relation, at once; she'd be the first one who should be told. She hurried to the telephone in the bar and dialled a familiar number quickly.

"Mrs Watson? It's Betty Fletcher from the pub … No, I'm well thank you. Mrs Watson, I have terrible news for you about your relation, Lady Emily … Yes, well … I'm sorry, but she's dead … Yes … but… she's been … *murdered*! …

"No, I can't really believe it either. Stephen Armitage found the body, here, in the bar room …You'll be over? Thank you; I thought you should be the first one to know … Thank you; see you soon."

***

Annie stood at the telephone table in shock. Well, everyone was wishing the woman dead, and now she is! But, merciful God … murdered! The worst part of it is that I cannot even feel sorry for the woman! God forgive me and God have mercy on the soul of that demented woman.

As the shock began to subside, Annie's shrewd, intelligent brain began ticking over. If there's a murder, then there will be suspects. *Suspects*!

That's about two-thirds of the entire village!

Wait a minute, what did Amelia say she was going to do? Oh, my God, it's not possible is it? Harriet also had threatened to take to Emily. Good God, so had Thelma Kemp and Laura in their anguish, over Mr and Mrs Nicholls.

There's Dan Kelly as well and, of course, Stephen himself – he found the body. He'd be the first to be suspected; he had also said something had to be done about that evil woman.

Oh, what *should* she do?

She thought the first sensible thing to do would be to make sure that all the people know about her death; then, in a secret part of Annie's mind, came the thought that this would give people time to work out their alibis.

When she became aware of what she was actually thinking, she was filled with guilt; she actually blushed with shame; she was already condoning murder in her mind – a terrible sin.

Well, she could try to atone for that by just letting the people know. She reached for the phone. Now, who needs to know? There's Harriet, Laura, Hannah and, of course, Amelia, but Amelia doesn't have a phone. I'll catch up with her going to the pub.

***

Twenty minutes later, a group of people were approaching the pub – mainly women but young Dan Kelly and Tim Johnson, were there as well.

Annie met the group on the steps and after various greetings, exclamations of astonishment and horror were exchanged, they entered the pub doors and found Betty guarding the entrance to the bar room.

The landlord and his wife were standing in the hall foyer looking frightened and anxious. They welcomed Annie with relief; she immediately went to them and kissed them. She stood with them and listened to the babble of questions from the others.

"Mr Jones," Annie asked, "have the police been called?"

"Yes, Miss Anne," the elderly man replied. "They're in the bar room now, with the body; no one is allowed to go in …"

"No, I suppose not. Where is Stephen Armitage? He found the body, didn't he?"

"He's in there with the police, Miss Anne."

"But what happened?" queried Harriet McKenzie.

Mr Jones looked even more distressed. "I simply don't know, Mrs McKenzie. The Lady Emily said she was going to stay quietly, in the alcove seat near the window, all day; said she was feeling poorly.

"I noticed her as I went in and out, but I didn't pay much attention. She could have gone out, for all I know."

"Did she have drinks during the day," Laura Hennessy asked. "If she was murdered, then I imagine she was poisoned … or wasn't she?"

"I don't know that either." Mr Jones looked even more distressed. "Oh, dear, I hope it wasn't poison Mrs Hennessy; people will think it came from the drinks here!" He turned towards the bar and called to Betty Fletcher. "Betty, did Lady Emily drink much during the day?"

"No, she didn't, Mr Jones," Betty replied without leaving her post at the door. "I served her with a bottle of soda water and a glass this morning, and about an hour later, she asked for a gin and tonic. That was all she had to my knowledge.

"Oh course, I had many tasks to do today and when the bar's not open, I'm hardly in the bar room at all. She could have helped herself to anything, if she wanted it."

"Has she done that before, Betty?" Dan Kelly asked.

"As a matter of fact, Dan, no, she hasn't. She drank very little alcohol – perhaps a glass of wine with her dinner, but that was about all. The other one – the 'Russian' – actually likes a glass or two. She mainly drinks whiskey and gin-tonics."

The group continued to speculate and various theories were put forward. Annie, though appealed to several times, remained silent. She had a fearful sensation of remorse – of guilt; she had disliked this woman intensely; thought her an evil woman, but had never, never ever, in her life, wished anyone dead.

Annie was scrupulously honest; she realised that everyone would be glad that Emily, was dead – which was a terrible, terrible thing.

God was the final judge; no one else. She looked at her feet and twisted her hands together in her mental anguish.

The group became aware of her distress and the noise gradually quietened. There was a sudden silence in the hall; Annie's neighbours were embarrassed for her.

The uneasy silence was broken in a gruesome manner. Above their heads the group heard a light female musical voice singing tunefully, a ditty she had heard, on the wireless:

"And, la, la, de-doo, de-doo,

A boy, a girl with her kangaroo,

Wed in a place called Gundaru,

And all the folks said how de do ..."

The singing broke off. Lady Emily looked down, at the assembled group of people, smiled graciously, and swept down the rest of the stairs.

There were startled gasps of something akin to terror, from the women, and oaths from the men. They stared speechless in horror, at the apparition on the stairs.

"What a lovely surprise," Lady Emily cried, "and Annie, too! Dressed to kill as usual! – you really must tell me your dressmaker!"

Lady Emily let loose her tinkling musical laugh. "But what on earth is the occasion? What has happened? I cannot believe that something of importance has occurred, in your so quaint, little, hamlet!" She fluttered her little hands.

"Come on, now don't be coy, pray, do tell."

Annie felt the whole room moving; I am going to faint, she thought. She grabbed on to Joe Jones' solid arm. He was equally horrified and patted her hand, abstractedly. The terrified silence that had engulfed everybody was broken by Laura Hennessy.

She swallowed hastily, and spoke with her voice shaking:

"But, it can't be ... you're, you're ..." she began, and promptly fainted. Laura's neighbours rushed to help her.

"I don't understand," Lady Emily raised her beautifully sculpted eyebrows and opened her eyes wide.

Amelia Tatley strode forward and stood in front of Emily.

"Tell us: who is the corpse in the other room?" she demanded fiercely. Lady Emily took a step backward, at the threatening tone of Amelia's voice.

"Corpse?"

"Yes, the murdered woman."

"Murdered?"

"Yes, murdered. You see, we all thought it was *YOU*." Amelia turned her back and returned to stand, defiantly, next to Annie.

Lady Emily positively beamed with pleasure.

"And you came here to *grieve* together, did you? How unbelievably *sweet*! And my own relation, too! I bet *she* was distraught over my 'death.'"

Lady Emily laughed merrily. "It really is so sweet of all of you; I did not really think you cared and all the time you were ready to *wake* for me – how terribly feudal – I must write to tell my friends about it – they'll find it hilarious!"

Dan Kelly had had enough of this. He thrust himself to the doorway to the bar.

"Inspector Peters," he shouted, "please, just tell us the *name* of the woman who's been murdered. We all thought it was this bitch here, called Lady Emily."

Annie moved quickly to Dan, and whispered: "Dan, be careful what you say. This is a murder enquiry now …" Inspector Peters' voice interrupted her. He appeared briefly at the doorway.

"Good morning everyone. I'll be with you in a moment. I'll need those of you who came to the pub today to wait – you especially, Lady Emily …"

"Good gracious Inspector, why on earth do you want me? I won't even know the woman …"

"I don't think there's much danger of you, not knowing her – it's your companion, Miss Tanya Illich."

"No!" shrieked Lady Emily. "Let me through to her. Immediately! How dare you try to stop me, Inspector; I'll report you! Get
out of my way, you low-bred clot! You …"

Lady Emily swooned prettily and gracefully and before he could
get out of the way, Inspector Peters found himself supporting this
woman he despised, in his arms. As quickly as he could, his face
grimacing, he lowered her body to the floor, left her there and
returned to the crime scene.

CHAPTER 12

"Did you take down Captain Armitage's statement, Pierce?" Inspector Peters asked his sergeant brusquely. "You did? Right! Captain Armitage you can go on home now; I'm sure Mrs Armitage will be anxious about you. I'll be dropping in to see you later."

Stephen Armitage nodded, and prepared to leave, as Peters added softly: "Thank you Stephen, for getting us so promptly – that was a lucky break."

The ambulance had gone, and taken the body with it; the police surgeon had likewise examined the body and declared that – as anyone with half a brain could see – it was a clear case of cyanide poisoning.

While there, he had looked briefly at Lady Emily and, without any fuss, dumped her on a chair in a corner of the room and pushed her head down between her knees. Reviving quickly with this treatment, Peters had then placed her in the little office Mr Jones had made available to him.

The scientific team had carefully dusted everything for prints and found, as they said, 'thousands," which was useless to the inspector, while the broken glass had been carefully collected. The team indicated it was fairly confident, the glass had held the poison, from which the woman had drunk.

Peters sat down near the table where Tanya had sat. He wondered vaguely how the titled lady was getting on, sitting in that bleak little office – without even a fire. The inspector had arranged for tea to be served to Lady Emily, but she had been left completely alone; he knew she would not be pleased with *that*.

Constable Manders, his young handsome face serious, had arrived and at Peters direction, had taken the names of all those who had been in the hall foyer when the Inspector had arrived.

They had then been allowed to return to their homes. In fact, the policemen knew all of them well; he knew there was no danger of them fleeing the area – they were all locals.

Now that the first part of the 'business' had been completed, Peters sat, troubled and weary, with his long-time colleague, Sergeant Pierce and the young Constable, Manders. He suddenly remembered one of the Constables.

"Pierce," he demanded, "where the hell is Potts? He was with us, at the beginning."

The sergeant smiled. "He's with the landlord and his wife in the kitchen, sir. He said that he'd have a chat with them – he's known them forever – he'll see if they can tell him which of the locals have been in and out of the pub, today."

"Good idea. He's a sensible man – with a nose for the right scent every time." Peters sighed. "Well, come on, Pierce, what are your thoughts on this one?"

"I think it's fairly clear, sir. The wrong person was murdered."

"Well, it seems like that, but we must be careful …'

"Lady Emily did tell both the publican and Betty, that she was going to stay at the seat near the window for the day, didn't she?" Pierce cut in.

"Yes, but she could have left at any time, with Tanya taking her place."

Manders cleared his throat. "Sir, are you thinking in terms of an accidental death. That is, with Miss Illich not the intended victim, but the Lady Emily?"

"Well, it certainly looks like that, but we must not discount the fact that Tanya Illich may have aroused such fury, by her pamphlets and bolshie propaganda, that someone actually killed the person they intended."

Sergeant Pierce was not convinced. "That leaves the problem of the cyanide, sir. To me, if the poisoner is a local, just where did they get hold of such a drug?"

"Excuse me again, Sergeant," intervened the constable, "didn't someone say that the two ladies had aroused great anger down at the hospital? I was thinking of drugs you see."

"I hope to hell you're wrong, son," Peters observed. "I don't think I could get through another murder investigation at the hospital. However, it's early days yet." He straightened up in his chair. "When we finish the next interview, we'll beg a cup of tea from Mrs Jones. I know I need it, what about you, Pierce?"

"Too right. I can still smell that horrible almond smell, from the corpse."

"That was actually interesting, Pierce – I was surprised at that. Often, they say, it's impossible to smell any almonds at all, with cyanide poisoning. I'm an amateur in that area, but I *think* it might indicate that a huge amount of the drug was used in the drink. If that's right, then it adds more difficulty to the problem. Ah, well! I can't put it off any longer. I have to see Lady Emily. But first, I have a job for you Manders."

"Sir?"

"Go and join Potts and tell him I want you both to go to the Quarry area to sound out the people there. I believe that this Illich woman spent most of her time – with her propaganda – in that area.

"See what the locals actually thought of her; whether any of them were aroused to such fury, by the pamphlets that they would injure her. That sort of thing – tell Potts, he'll know the drill."

"Certainly, sir, I'll go to Constable Potts in the kitchen now."

"Join us Constable, here at the pub, when you're finished."

"Sir."

"Come on Pierce – I can't put it off any longer. Now for the Lady Emily."

***

As Peters and Pierce entered the small private room, Lady Emily was found sitting rigidly staring blankly at the opposite wall. For once, her beautifully applied makeup, failed to hide the fact that she was not a young woman. It was a surprise, to the policemen, to see her without that supercilious false smile on those expertly painted lips.

Without a word, the two men sat at the table opposite the woman. Peters waited for her to break the silence. He didn't have to wait long.

"Is it possible that the fact has actually entered your bucolic heads, that I was the intended victim?" Sergeant Pierce clenched his lips tight shut to prevent him speaking. Really, the unbelievable arrogance of this woman!

"Believe it or not, Lady Emily," Inspector Peters answered mildly, "yes, it has entered our considerations. But we didn't think you were of sufficient importance to warrant anyone murdering you!"

Lady Emily actually gasped. Her mouth fell open. She rallied herself to speak, but Peters deliberately got in first.

"But, with Miss Illich, *there* is someone very important. She would have many enemies with all her propaganda; I believe several families, with sons fighting abroad, will be delighted to have her dead. Whereas, with you? Really, who would really be interested?"

Lady Emily rushed into speech.

"You fool! Don't you know that Harriet McKenzie is after my blood, simply because I broke off the engagement between George and Penelope Watson. It wasn't suitable for a relative of mine to be marrying a McKenzie."

"You're actually implying that Harriet McKenzie felt so strongly about this that she'd kill you? Frankly, that's ridiculous."

"Well, what about my loving cousin, Annie Watson? She loathes me. Just because I exposed that wicked, depraved Dr Scott and thus her pathetic Billy – a gangling scarecrow of a boy, with the brains of a peasant – lost his tutor for the matriculation examination – as if he'd ever pass it, in the first place!" Emily warmed to her theme.

"Yes, Annie is a prime suspect. She's a leader here in this ghastly hole – the others do exactly what she tells them to do. And look at her! Looks like a tramp, dresses like a Balkan peasant, has hands that are red and callused and, as for her shoes! Words *fail* me!"

"What a blessing that is, at any rate," agreed the Inspector. "While you are venting your spleen, are there by any chance any others in the village, who are after your blood?" Peters laughed, to indicate that such an idea was ridiculous.

"Is your name Constable *Plod*? Of *course* there are! Laura Hennessy would kill me as quick as a flash, if she could get away with it, just because I made sure she knew that her sweet, demure, daughter, Joan was flirting disgustingly with the soldiers up at the Red Cross Hospital at The Junction. And I made sure I told her fiancé, Dan Kelly, all about it."

"So, we can add Laura Hennessy's name to the list, with Dan Kelly too, can we?"

"Yes, you can, and write down, as well, that stuck-up nothing called Thelma Kemp – gives herself airs, just because she's the *doctor's* wife. God help us! A *doctor's* wife!"

"And just why would Thelma Kemp be interested in bumping you off?"

"I detest those American expressions! 'Bumping off', so vulgar, and just what I would expect from the police here." Lady Emily raised her voice.

"Of *course*, Thelma Kemp is a strong suspect. She blames me for the deaths of Major Denis Nicholls and his wife."

"Goodness, how did you manage that?"

"I didn't kill them, you idiot! But these women say I caused it."

"How?"

"Well, I happen to know an expert in Military History and I discussed Major Nicholls' campaign in the Boer War with him ..." Lady Emily paused to laugh in real amusement.

"Campaign! More like a horrible slaughter of his men, from his own incompetence. I bearded him in his study, told him I knew all about it and intended to give the story to the newspapers."

Peters looked away from the woman for a moment. Was it possible this woman was sane? He doubted it. Or perhaps, could she be evil? Yes, that's more like it, he thought. She glories in her deeds ... and she knows, full well, what she's doing.

He forced himself to look back at her, his eyes cold. He put one hand under the table, and patted Pierce's knee reassuringly; he could actually feel the Sergeant about to explode, at any moment.

"Well, that's quite a line up of suspects. Have you finished yet?"

"No, I haven't, and you'll find it expedient to pay attention to me, Inspector Peters. I am not without influence, I have ..."

"Please don't bore me, Lady Emily. I know all about you. I know your nephew Dr Gascoigne-Ridley well ... we were talking about suspects."

"Well, have you thought of that desiccated spinster, Amelia Tatley? She has a real reason for silencing me. She actually came to see me this morning, and actually threatened me! *She* threatened *ME!*"

"A lovely elderly lady, Miss Amelia Tatley, I've always thought ..."

"A lovely lady! What would you say if I told you that I know she actually was once in jail?"

"Quite frankly, I wouldn't believe it. Anyone else? I want to have a cup of tea, so let's get this rigmarole of the suspects over and done with, shall we?"

"There are the Armitages – they would be near the top of my list. What a pair! The husband's a mental case ... and the wife! Dear heaven … the wife! Has she given up soliciting yet, do you happen to know?"

The Inspector stood up and motioned Pierce to do the same.

"I have noted your comments, Madam, and I shall be speaking to you later today. You may go to your room, but you are forbidden to leave the building; if you attempt to do so, I shall arrest you. Good morning." He turned abruptly and left the room followed by Pierce.

"Sssh! Pierce! Not a word, lad. Let's go to the kitchen."

***

As the policemen came through the kitchen door they surprised Mr Jones, his wife Biddy and Betty, at the table having their lunch.

Peters quickly excused himself and backed out of the room. Mr Jones sprang to his feet, hurried to the hall, and invited the two men to join them for lunch, apologizing that it would only be at the kitchen table.

Inspector Peters hastened to say that he and Pierce would be honoured to eat with their old friends, so within a few minutes, both men were seated at the table, enjoying a simple meal of sandwiches and fruit.

They were glad to see that Mrs Jones had made a large pot of tea; they were longing for a cup.

At the table, talk was of the great shock this whole affair had been to the elderly landlord and his wife and especially to Betty. Mr Jones was worried about Betty who, once again, had to stand guard, until the police took over.

"My dear Betty," Peters said between large bites of his sandwich, "you seem destined to be one of the first to receive the shocks of murdered bodies, here in Bexford North."

"It's all your fault, Inspector," smiled Betty, pouring the tea, "since you and Sergeant Pierce came to our area, we've had nothing but dead bodies turning up everywhere. I led quite an uneventful life before you came."

The policemen laughed gently. Peters looked ruefully at the young woman. "Betty, I'll never forgive myself for asking you to take that message down to the Reserve last year; I never dreamt you would find what you did."

"Well, that's over and done with, thank God," Betty answered. "Yes, it was a great shock – far more than this one. This one was more … *bewildering*, I think."

"That makes sense to me," Pierce spoke up. "You thought one woman was dead and then discovered that it was another person altogether."

"That's it, exactly, Sergeant. I simply couldn't understand it. When Captain Armitage came in and asked for Lady Emily, I automatically pointed to the alcove table; that was where I last saw her. The Captain went across there and discovered her *companion* – not Lady Emily – and what's more, found her dead!"

"Was he very badly shocked, Betty," the inspector asked quickly. "The very last thing I would want, is that he'd have a relapse after what he's been through." Betty stopped eating and stared into space, remembering.

"Yes, he was badly shocked, but no, I don't think there's been damage done. He seems to have recovered quickly, anyhow. He must have remembered seeing your car down at his place, for he suddenly tore out of the room, and we nearly had another disaster."

"Oh?"

"I was carrying a very large tray of newly washed glasses through the door at the time. I saw Stephen just in time; turned slightly aside and called out. He paused, and I managed to get the tray onto the counter of the bar. We could easily have had glass everywhere."

"A lucky result," agreed the Inspector. "Betty, were there many people here to see Lady Emily this morning?"

"Were there ever! It seemed as if half the village came to see her sitting there at the window seat. I saw a couple of them, but I was only in the bar room, now and then, as my work dictated."

"Can you remember who came first, Betty? I'm sorry to ask you these questions in your lunch break. Would you prefer we wait until later?"

"Definitely not," Betty answered firmly. 'It's fresh in my mind now; if I leave it to later I'll not be sure of what I'm telling you."

"That's a sensible approach and no mistake," applauded Peters. He turned to the landlord. "Mr Jones, you have a good and reliable helper here in your pub."

"And always has been, Inspector, ever since she first came here. I told mother that this was the one who would not only stay, but would be the one that we could depend on."

Mrs Jones nodded her head vigorously and urged the policemen to have another cup of tea. Betty was again staring into space, thinking; finally she spoke.

"I think the order was this: first came Harriet McKenzie – went to the window seat, I pointed it out to her; didn't stay long. Next came Laura Hennessy – she found Lady Emily herself – I wasn't in the room when she arrived; didn't stay long either.

"Next came Dan Kelly and Bianca Firelli – I must have been there, as I told them where the woman was. Dan and Bianca stayed a fair while – I was surprised how long it was actually.

"Thelma Kemp came next – I didn't see her until she was leaving. Must have been a stormy meeting, for Thelma was red in the face, when I caught a glimpse of her, in the vestibule, as she was going out of the pub."

For the first time, Betty hesitated. Peters was immediately alert.

"What is it, Betty? You realise that just coming to see Lady Emily, is no crime in itself. It doesn't mean that I'm going to rush off and arrest somebody, just because they happened to be unfortunate enough to have visited that pestilential woman, on the day her companion was murdered."

"You're right, of course," Betty said slowly, "but I'm frightened of accidentally putting someone on the spot; someone who had a motive, and yet is innocent ..."

"If it's of any help to you, Betty, there'd be hardly a single person in this village, who didn't have a motive for murdering Lady Emily."

"I suppose you're right," Betty sighed. "All right – next to come, was Major Tim Johnson – a particular friend of mine ..."

"And of mine too, Betty," quickly added Peters.

"Yes, that's true. Well, Tim had a crazy idea of how he thought he could get the two women to leave the area; he'd already spoken to Tanya, so this morning he came to see Lady Emily.

"I wasn't there when he came in, nor when he left – I was needed with the linen upstairs. Mr Jones told me later he'd been here; I didn't see him at all. " Mr Jones nodded.

Betty continued: "Next time I was in the bar room, I saw Amelia Tatley standing in front of Emily's table. They seemed to be arguing hotly – but I don't know what about; I only heard Amelia's voice."

"And she was the last was she, Betty?"

"No, just as she was leaving the front lobby, Stephen Armitage arrived ... And you know what happened next."

"Indeed, we do. Thank you Betty, that was unbelievably helpful." He placed his elbows on the table and pushed the tea cup aside. "Now, would you tell me something else? What did you personally think of Tanya Illich?"

Betty was surprised; she was thoughtful for a few moments.

"Do you know what, Inspector? I *admired* her! There! I admired her for her guts. She believed completely, and firmly, in her new-found religion and would, I'm sure, have died for it. She also was a fighter ..." Betty started to laugh.

She then repeated the episode of the taunting by the children and the egg throwing.

"While the titled dame was throwing hysterics and rushing

upstairs to salvage her makeup, Tanya took herself out to the back tap, sluiced herself clean then came, sopping wet, deliberately to the bar room and demanded a drink.

"When I saw this, I thought this girl *has* something – despite all her pamphlets. I think she was a brave – indeed, a courageous – woman."

"That's very interesting and helpful, Betty." Peters then addressed the landlord. "Mr Jones what did you think of Miss Tanya Illich?"

Joe Jones rubbed his jaw thoughtfully. "Well, Inspector, I have to say that I have no complaints to make about her, *as a guest*, of the hotel. She was always polite, courteous and quietly spoken; never complained of a single thing and, apart from her beliefs, caused us no trouble at all."

"And her beliefs, Mr Jones?"

The elderly man's face turned beetroot red with anger. "Dreadful! Simply wicked! How anyone, let alone a woman, could be sprouting such wicked ideas is beyond me – especially in our great suffering with this dreadful war!

"We have so many young boys – and girls too – from the village, serving in dreadful places overseas; some have been killed, some are in those dreadful prison camps – God alone knows if they'll ever get home … and these women …" Jim paused, "I'm sorry to say this, Inspector, but it seems to me that our system of Justice does not work fairly.

"These two women should have been shot as traitors! There! That's what I think."

"You feel strongly, Mr Jones, and so do I," remarked Peters, "unfortunately we can do nothing. I'm interested to hear you blame Lady Emily, as much as Miss Illich?"

"Well, I do. She ought to know better. Her with all the money in the world; with clothes that cost a fortune on her back, talking about workers' rights! Such hypocrisy! It's laughable that's what it is. Of the two, I think worse of her, than of the young woman.

"Young men and women get all sorts of rubbishy ideas in their heads, but most grow out of them in a few years. But Lady Emily! She must be over forty if she's a day and the damage she's caused! Why, with the Liveridges alone ..." Mrs Jones quickly squeezed her husband's arm.

"What about the Liveridges, Mr Jones?" quickly asked Peters. "Mrs Liveridge works here doesn't she?"

"I'm sorry, Inspector," answered the landlord, his honest face frowning worriedly, "I shouldn't have mentioned them at all. It's nothing ..." He looked hard at the policemen.

"Gentlemen, I am not used to speaking badly of people. I know my place and I've kept it to the best of my ability all my life. I cannot understand why I suddenly sprouted all that bad talk about people who are actually guests in the hotel."

He stood up from the table. "If you'll excuse me gentlemen, I must get on with my work."

The policemen quickly took the hint, thanked Mrs Jones for a wonderful lunch and left the room. As they were walking back towards the little room they used, they heard themselves being called softly by Betty.

"Inspector, could we go into the little parlour for a moment?" Peters nodded and followed the young woman into the room. Betty stood near the door.

"No, I'll not sit, thank you, Inspector. I just wanted to explain about Mrs Liveridge. Both Mr and Mrs Jones are such totally good and decent people, that poor old Joe is now beside himself with guilt that he has let the cat out of the bag, as he thinks – he is such a faithful, kindly man."

"And, Betty, *you* realise, that we most probably know all about Bert Liveridge already," he spoke gently, "which, of course, we do.

"As a matter of fact, Constable Potts is up there in the Quarry road, this very minute, trying to get to the bottom of the Liveridge affair."

"Well, that's a relief," smiled Betty. "I didn't want you to think badly of old Joe. He's a good man."

Sergeant Pierce was curious. "Tell me, Betty, has Mrs Liveridge spoken to you about the situation with Bert, her husband."

"She has, Sergeant, the poor woman. She does the big washing-up here and helps with the cleaning. She was actually crying the other day – about the situation with her husband.

"Apparently, her neighbours, who have sons overseas, aren't talking to her, or are saying dreadful things to her, *because* of Bert taking up with Tanya.

"Lily Liveridge, Bert's wife, is a nice old woman and was truly upset. She has had to work hard all her life; her only friends have been her neighbours for decades; suddenly she finds herself isolated, because of her husband's beliefs. Lily has great affection for her neighbours' boys now in prison camps. Oh! It's so beastly unfair!"

"Has Bert been to the pub today, Betty?" Pierce asked.

"Yes, he has. He had to deliver some stuff for Mr Jones in his cart – or, so he said – and he came through to the bar for a beer. I was surprised to see him; he usually comes to the pub in the evening. I haven't seen him drink here in the daytime before. Anyway, I served him a beer and left the bar; I'd more things to do upstairs."

"Thank you Betty," Peters said, "for telling us about Mrs Liveridge. Now, we've taken up enough of your time, so off you go and thank you once again. You've been a tremendous help."

CHAPTER 13

The policemen sat at the table and studied the notes they had taken. Sergeant Pierce broke the silence. "Sir, from what Betty has told us, it seems that we have eight people who actually came to the pub this morning to see Lady Emily."

"Eight, is it?"

"I think so, if we discount Mr Liveridge – we don't know yet if he came to see her, or not. But, we do know that Harriet McKenzie, Laura Hennessy, Dan Kelly, Bianca Firelli, Thelma Kemp, Tim Johnson, Amelia Tatley and Stephen Armitage, *were* here."

"And what an unlikely lot of killers they are, eh, Pierce?"

"I agree, sir, but they *were* here …"

"I know, I know … but it all sounds so ridiculous." Peters got up and walked about the room. "The whole bloody thing sounds ridiculous. We have eight, or possibly more, suspects on the spot, all of whom had a motive for killing Lady *Emily* and what happens? We have the *wrong corpse!*"

"I agree, sir. It's the cyanide that beats me every time. How did these people get hold of cyanide? Oh course, there's Major Tim Johnson – perhaps he could get it from the hospital, but would they keep cyanide there?" Pierce grimaced. "You'd hardly expect that to be prescribed for the sick soldiers, would you?"

"We might know more when the autopsy report arrives, Pierce, though it's clear it's definitely hydrogen cyanide."

"You know I don't want it to be Captain Armitage, sir, but he *was* the last one to arrive it seems."

"And the last one to arrive is, so often, the one who turns out to be the murderer. Or, the one who 'discovers' the murder, is often the killer. But we have a problem here with that, Pierce; he would have seen it was Tanya, and *not* Lady Emily, sitting in the window seat."

"Why would he want to kill Tanya Illich?" He looked to the door. "Yes, Betty, what is it?"

"It's Mrs Watson, sir. She asked if she might have a word with you; said she won't keep you a moment."

"Of course. Please send her in, Betty."

Annie hurried in looking harassed and troubled. "Good morning gentlemen. I won't keep you a moment – I know how busy you are."

Peters made Annie sit down. He noticed the severe lines of strain on her face.

"Mrs Watson, this has been a terrible week for everyone, but especially for you, as it was your relative that was involved. Please believe me that I understand the anguish you have been through, especially with Billy."

"Well, thanks be to God, Inspector, once again, it seems as if Billy is going to weather the shock. That's something to be thankful for; what we are to do about the tutoring, is another matter." She shook her head impatiently.

'But, that's my problem, not yours – you have enough – I didn't come to talk about my problems. Gentlemen, I don't know if you're aware, but Dr Ernest Gascoigne-Ridley is coming here this afternoon."

"Oh, Lord!"

"Exactly. That's why I thought I'd better come to warn you. He's due at the Convalescent Hospital this afternoon. I had to contact him, about poor Dr Scott giving up the tutoring and he promised to come and see the poor chap. You see," Annie added miserably, "I don't think he even knows yet the poor man is dead – or, *how* he died. Or … who was *responsible*, for Harry taking his own life."

"You didn't contact him after Captain Scott's death?"

"No, Inspector, I should have, but I simply forgot, in all the shock."

"Very understandable. Look, he will undoubtedly be coming to the pub, to see his aunt, so I could fill him in on the developments – and explain about Dr Scott."

"He'll be upset. Harry Scott was a friend of his."

"Oh dear! However, we'll manage. Do you want him to call and see you?"

"I don't think that's fair to ask of him; he's a fearfully busy man and he's got all the worry of that woman, on top of everything."

"Well, we'll see what he thinks. You know, Mrs Watson, I find it hard to believe that so much damage has been done to so many people's lives by one woman, in just a few days."

"And everyone in the village hated her. Isn't that awful! This morning, coming here thinking she was dead, I was guilt-ridden, for not feeling sorry that she *was* dead. Yet all the time, it was that poor young woman – who was no trouble really to anyone – who was hideously murdered, in mistake for Emily."

"You were not upset about Tanya Illich's activities?"

"Well, it was all so silly, really. No one in the village, except perhaps the village atheist, Bert Liveridge, even took it seriously. I think we – all the women, anyhow – felt that we had enough on our hands, just trying to survive and be able to put food on the table.

"We had no time, nor interest in, Communist Ideology. Mind you, I think the poor young woman was genuine enough; I think she believed in it, as the Gospel."

"That's the interesting thing, Mrs Watson. We keep hearing that assessment of Tanya Illich. I'm actually inclined to believe it. When talking to Tanya myself, I gained the impression, however misguided she was, by her own lights she was an honest woman."

"I think you'll find that was the impression most people had of her. Personally, I just felt sorry for her. When you're young, it's easy to be swept up in movements, that you are convinced will save the world.

"Tanya, I believe, truly thought she was doing something that had never even been thought of before, yet the idea of the Utopian society has been around for ever." Annie smiled sadly at the two men.

"I think the whole Russian experiment will end in fearful disillusionment, and involve horrendous suffering, as all Uptopias end up in dictatorships eventually."

She stood up. "Must get back to Billy, Inspector," Annie nodded to Sergeant Pierce. 'Please apologize for me to Ernest, when he comes; I should have contacted him – Harry being a close friend." Annie shook hands, absently, with both men and hurried from the room.

Peters sighed. "This is another rotten case, Pierce. Let's get organized. I wonder how much longer Potts and Manders are going to be ..."

"I heard a car a little while ago; I think you'll find that's them now, sir," the door opened. "Yes, here they are."

"Come in, chaps and tell me who actually did the murder, and all the gossip you've picked up." Peters looked closely at his men. "I was going to ask if you were hungry, but I see you've eaten."

"Now, how did you know that, sir," smiled young Manders.

"It's why they made me a detective, son," Peters replied. "No, to tell the truth I see some pickle stains on Potts' tie, and I can distinctly smell pickled onions on your breath. Ergo, I deduce that you had corned beef sandwiches with pickles."

Constable Potts laughed, and ruefully examined his tie. "You see, young Manders, you can't get away with anything, with this boss!" All the men laughed, and the newcomers settled themselves round the table to begin their reports.

"You first, Constable Potts," ordered Peters.

"Well, sir, not a great lot to report, however we've covered a fair bit of ground. We went most places together, as Manders is not well known out here. Now for the Quarry people." Potts again settled himself comfortably. "Only one case of interest and that was ..."

"Bert Liveridge," intervened Sergeant Pierce.

"Right again, Sarge. Yes, he's a person of interest – to himself, more than to anyone else, I think.

"Regarding the deceased, everyone except Bert Liveridge, thought she was a deluded woman, and that her doctrines were dangerous, indeed wicked, but, strangely enough, thought Tanya, herself, was an honest and decent woman, who believed all she was sprouting."

"And Lady Emily?"

"There you have another kettle of fish, Inspector. Everyone fairly hated her, they did! They were mainly disappointed that she wasn't the corpse. They shut their doors in her face, whenever she came to see them."

"That really surprises me, Potts, seeing as how she was related to the famous and never to be forgotten, Sheridans."

"Again, sir, that's just the point. This silly woman set them all against her, in the beginning by bad-mouthing Annie Watson – Lady Mary Sheridan's daughter – as soon as she entered their houses."

"Bad-mouthing her, in what way, Potts," enquired Pierce.

"You know, sir: her poor clothes, her untidiness, her poverty, her work-roughened hands and then Lady Emily, stupidly, began on Billy."

"She didn't!" Sergeant Pierce was scandalized.

"She did! She said he was a 'poseur' – is that the right word? – that there was nothing the matter with him – that his mother pretended that he had brains but actually he was mentally deficient, and if that was not enough, she hinted that there was something bad – sexually – going on between Billy and the poor Dr Scott." Potts scratched his ear.

"The people in the Quarry think the world of Annie Watson and are very fond of Billy as well, so you can imagine how *that* went down."

"Dear God! Is there no end to the infamy of this woman!" exclaimed Peters.

"It seems not, sir. Anyhow, the good people of the Quarry, had her out of their houses as quickly as they decently could. She was never invited back in again – even to Bert Liveridge's house."

"Very informative, Potts. You've just added about another twenty, or more, people to our list of suspects," Peters concluded wryly. "Not to worry; tell me about Bert. What do you really think of him?

"Is he a possible suspect do you think, Potts? I can tell you, he was here at the pub, for a short time this morning, but I have no proof that he either saw, or spoke, to the dead girl."

"At the pub, eh? Must have been a quick call! Well, Bert Liveridge. I've known him a long time, sir and he's always been, what we used to call, a 'bit bolshie'.

"You know, complaining all the time about how down-trodden we were; that we were just wage-slaves; that our Masters were no better than we were; that, by rights, we should have all the good things the Upper Classes have; and he's always had a thing about inequality of education.

"I think, sir," Potts added shrewdly, 'the truth is, that actually Bert, is an intelligent man – old now, of course – and would have loved to have had a really, good education. Always wanted to *know* things … you know what I mean.

"But regarding this murder, no, I don't really think so. He certainly was very keen on money of course, but if he did anything for money, it'd have to be something he believed in – he has a sort of integrity in that regard.

"I'm assuming you mean did he do it under the impression he was bumping off the *Emily woman*, for he had no reason to kill

Tanya. He admired her; she was on the right track; she said all the things he had been saying for years and no one would take any notice of him.

"He never stopped saying what a wonderful woman she was and was furious that she was the one who was killed. Said we, the police, were an effete and useless adjunct to the ruling classes; we were only used to prop up a decaying and useless, class structure." Potts started to laugh. "So there, sir, that's what we are!"

"Thank you, Potts, I am suitably chastened. I must learn to keep my place more humbly. But, seriously Potts, I want you to bring Bert Liveridge in for questioning; I am very puzzled about something that doesn't make sense.

"I'm sorry, Potts, I should have thought of this earlier – would've saved you a trip back there. All right? Do that when we finish here."

He turned to Manders who was smiling broadly. "Now you young whippersnapper, I take it you did something other than stuff yourself with food at ... let me guess: Hannah Kelly's place?"

"Right on the button, sir," laughed Constable Manders. "I think I did earn my salary. Let me see. Constable Potts gave me the market gardeners – the Firellis – and then, the Kellys to do on my own. I had some trouble with the Italian family – they are anti-police, on account of their men-folk being interned. However, one of the daughters – a beautiful girl, sir – Bianca, her name was – admitted that she and Dan did come to see Lady Emily.

"She finally also admitted, that they had come to tell her exactly what they thought of her."

"What did they basically have against her?" asked Pierce.

"They regarded her as responsible for the breaking off of the engagement between Dan Kelly and the Hennessy girl, Joan. They told me all about that.

"Then Bianca, whom I expect has a fairly fiery temper, took on the lady over her comments that, being Italians, they would naturally favour the Communist Party.

"Apparently, that was a grievous insult. The Firellis pride themselves on the fact that they are three-generation-Australians and are fiercely and proudly religious – Catholic, in fact, and Communism is atheistic.

"The two young people claimed that they saw Lady Emily together, at about a quarter to ten o'clock this morning. According to them, they had their argument – which Bianca admitted was fairly heated – and left the lady alive at about ten o'clock.

"As they were leaving, they saw Thelma Kemp come into the bar room. I asked about the glass on the table; Bianca said she noticed it; it was about half full. She thought it looked like soda water."

Peters wondered aloud about the Firellis. "They've got a real gripe; they've been treated very badly by the Government in interning those good men and they have fiery tempers. Doesn't make a lot of sense, though ..."

"If I may interrupt, sir," Manders coughed apologetically, "could I add something that occurred after I went to the Kelly house? It actually helps Dan and Bianca."

Peters nodded. Manders went on. "Well, I heard practically the very same words from Dan – strong young bloke, isn't he? It was only when I was leaving, that Mrs Kelly had a private word with me. She told me she thinks that Lady Emily had done Dan, a great favour.

"She thinks it has brought to Dan's notice, that right next door, he has a very lovely young girl who obviously is very keen on him. I think Mrs Kelly distinctly hears wedding bells chiming, in the near distance, but *not* with Joan Hennessy walking down the aisle, dressed in white, with flower-girls strewing rose petals, in front of her."

Constable Potts rolled his eyes. "Very colourful indeed, Constable; cut out the frills or I'll 'rose-petal' you and no mistake!"

Potts turned to his superior. "Sir, I've tried my best, but what can you do with the young chaps they're sending us today? I think it's the Pictures they see – they're the ruination of young coppers." Both Peters and Pierce chuckled. Peters then turned again to Manders.

"Constable, did Dan or, even Bianca, seem worried, anxious, fearful, or seemed afraid of saying too much?"

"Exactly the opposite, sir. I had the greatest difficulty in stopping the flow. They didn't exhibit the slightest signs of guilt, if that's what you mean, sir."

"Good, what else?"

"Nothing much. I joined Constable Potts in the Quarry area, and then we both returned to Kellys for lunch. I had promised Mrs Kelly I would go and find the Constable." Manders' eyes twinkled. "It was a very good lunch too."

Peters sorted through the notes he had made. He then sent Potts to collect Bert Liveridge, then began to organize, with Sergeant Pierce, the villagers that must be questioned – using the lists they had made previously.

"Sergeant I want you to take Constable Manders with you to these people," Peters instructed Piece. "Tell them to be at the pub tomorrow morning, at nine o'clock, but Pierce, be tactful, won't you? These good people are all well known to us – don't let them think we regard them as murderers – although, of course, it's possible one of them, may well be – but be polite, courteous, and accommodating.

"Try to give the impression that it is not all that important, but nevertheless, I want to see them here. You understand what I mean?"

Pierce nodded. "Let me just get these names clear, sir. There's Harriet McKenzie, Laura Hennessy, Thelma Kemp, Amelia Tatley, Major Tim Johnson, Dan Kelly, Bianca Firelli, and Captain Stephen Armitage – yes, that's right, eight people."

"Let's hope to God that after the interviews tomorrow, we can cut that number down considerably, Pierce. OK? Off you both go, and when you're finished, you can head off home.

"When Potts brings Bert Liveridge in to me, he can go too. I'll see Lady Emily's nephew when he arrives, and then catch the bus home.

"I'll stay as long as I can; I'm hoping that the autopsy report will be phoned through before I leave. I'll see you tomorrow, here at the pub, before the suspects arrive."

Pierce and Manders left, and Peters sat thinking about Bert Liveridge – there's something seriously wrong here, he thought, it doesn't make sense; why didn't he speak to her? There has to be a reason.

CHAPTER 14

Inspector Peters could hear Bert Liveridge long before he arrived in the small parlour.

A querulous voice was demanding whether, 'this was a fascist state'; whether he, 'should immediately go to the scaffold, as it was clear that they were going to charge him with a murder he did not commit, simply because he was a working man'; that, 'he had no rights, he knew that, with fascist pigs, which were what policemen were'.

The loud-voiced man was thrust roughly into the room, by Constable Potts, who told him bluntly to: 'shut his trap if he didn't want a bunch of fives in his face', which immediately provoked Bert into screaming loudly, of police brutality.

However, seeing the look on Potts' face, he hastily sat down at the table, facing Inspector Peters.

Peters looked coldly at the small man, in front of him. He noted the rough, working clothes and that the man was not very clean. However, Peters was aware, also, of the shrewd eyes that peered at him under thick bushy eyebrows.

Using a familiar technique of his, Peters sat in complete silence, staring coldly at the man. Eventually, Bert Liveridge could stand it no longer; beads of sweat began to form on his forehead and his partly-bald head.

"Well, I haven't got all day to waste sitting here. What are you waiting for?"

"I'm waiting for the truth, Mr Liveridge," Peters stated coldly.

"What do you mean, the truth? Truth about what?"

"You were here this morning, at the pub ..."

"So?"

"A young woman died ..."

"And a bloody fine and noble young woman, she was, too. You have to be joking to even think I had anything to do with her death."

"But I haven't even suggested that, Mr Liveridge. I don't think you had anything to do with her death."

"Well, why the bloody hell am I dragged here for questioning ..."

"Because I know you knew she was dead, when you were drinking your beer here, this morning ... Constable, quick! I think he's going to faint!"

Potts grabbed the elderly man and shoved his head, roughly, down between his knees. After a few moments, Bert with a trembling hand, took the glass of water that Potts handed him; slowly raising his head. The elderly constable spoke gently.

"Now, come on Bert, drink a little water. That's right. You've had a shock, that's all. You're all right."

Bert lifted the glass and drank the water with loud gulps, then forced himself to look at the inspector, all hostility gone.

"How did you know?" he gasped.

"It was pretty obvious, Mr Liveridge. You were great friends with the deceased; you have a chance to speak to her, which you didn't expect to have and then you expect me to believe that, coming into the bar room and finding her there, you didn't go to speak to her? Of course you went to speak to her and, to your horror, you found her dead.

"That's how it happened, didn't it."

The man nodded dumbly. "I got the shock of my life. You see Tanya was a real friend; she came to see me early this morning, about a certain matter and, worst luck, I was out, so I missed her.

"So, when I was asked to deliver some stuff to the pub, I hoped that I might be able to see her. The missus creates a treat if I have a drink in the mornings, but as she wasn't working at the pub today, I thought I'd have a quiet beer while I was here. I went into the bar and Betty drew me a beer, and then went away.

"At first I thought the woman in the window alcove was Lady Emily, but then I noticed something familiar – I think it must have been the thick stockings and the lace-up shoes.

"Anyhow, I realised it was Tanya. I hurried across to her and," his voice quavered, and he quickly drank more water, "to tell the truth, I nearly died of fright. One look at her, and I knew she was dead. I didn't know what to do …"

"Thank you, Mr Liveridge. That is exactly what I thought. Now, tell me, like a good chap. Do you have any idea of the time you saw Tanya?"

"I didn't really notice, Inspector. It must have been about eleven o'clock, or a little later, I think."

"Right. Tell me, did you touch the body at all? I am puzzled as to why it was still sitting up, resting against the back of the partition when the body was found. I think you moved the body, didn't you?"

Bert began to sweat again.

"Honest to God, Inspector, I didn't mean any harm. She was my friend, you see. Her head was lying on the table and I just couldn't believe that she could be dead.

"I lifted up her head gently by the hair and the body sort of fell back against the wooden partition. It made a hideous thud, which scared me to death.

"I got such a fright I got the hell out of the place, as quickly as I could and that's the god-awful truth! You've got to believe me!"

"As a matter of fact I do, Mr Liveridge. I never thought for a moment, that you killed Tanya. I'm sorry you moved the body; it was the wrong thing to do, but totally understandable in the circumstances. One thing more, Mr Liveridge," Peters added, "on your way out, did you notice anyone leaving, or entering, the bar room?"

"Only Stephen Armitage coming in the front way, as I was leaving by the back entrance – I don't think he saw me; I didn't see anyone else, not even Betty. She served me the drink when I first came in, but I didn't see her again."

Peters stood up. "Constable Potts will drive you home now, and as you have been treated with consideration and courtesy, you might reciprocate by showing courtesy to Constable Potts, who is a working man, just as much as you and I are. Good afternoon.

"Constable Potts when you have finished that task, you go home. Be back here tomorrow morning before nine."

***

An hour later, Betty knocked, and came into the parlour. "Inspector, there's a telephone call for you. You can take it in Mr Jones' office. The man said he was the police surgeon."

"Oh good, Betty. That'll be the autopsy report, thank you." Peters hurried to the phone.

"Thank you Doctor for letting me hear the results so quickly. Yes … I see, definitely hydrogen cyanide; no other signs of violence to body … Really? That's a large amount, isn't it? … I thought so. It's worried me from the beginning where the cyanide could have come from … You *KNOW*? …

"**WHAT? …NO!** *In the locket round her neck*! Are you joking with me? … No, I beg your pardon – of course you're not! I just can't believe it! It's the sort of stuff you see at the Pictures, but … Yes, I do remember it, small, insignificant … but, in what form would the cyanide be in the locket? … Oh, I see, and that would be soluble in liquid? Right! Could you tell me, Doctor, what would this thing have looked like? …I see, a capsule. How would you break it? …

Really? Usually between the *teeth!* … But, Doctor, please, *please*, just wait a minute; this changes the whole situation, doesn't it? …

"Yes, you're right, it looks like it was not murder at all, but *suicide*. Good God! This case will send me around the bend; this makes it even more incomprehensible … Yes, I beg your pardon, you're right, that's my problem, not yours … Yes, yes, thank you again Doctor, I do appreciate it."

Inspector Peters went into the bar, and sat on a stool at the furthest end. When Betty came to take his order, he said in a bitter tone: "A whisky, if you have any, Betty, and if possible, make it a large one."

As he slowly drank the whisky, Peters remembered that he still had to deal with the nephew of Lady Emily, the famous Dr Gascoigne-Ridley, and swore. Well, he thought, rebelliously, if he damn well smells drink on me, tough luck!

CHAPTER 15

Inspector Peters found, to his relief, that his meeting with Dr Ernest Gascoigne-Ridley was shorter, than he had anticipated.

The doctor, dressed in his usual impeccable fashion, was grave and unsmiling, his whole being sombre. He advanced on Peters and shook his hand vigorously.

"I always look forward to our meetings, Inspector. It appals me that it has to be under these atrocious circumstances. Firstly, let me say you have my complete and unaffected sympathy, for having to deal with the detritus that my aunt has caused, as usual.

"Nothing you could say, or even think, about that woman, would equal what I have thought, or said about her, over the past few years. She leaves behind her a trail of destruction – truly she is unique – I know of no other woman to cause so much trouble …"

Peters held up his hand. "Please, Doctor, I beg of you not to go on. Yes, Lady Emily has caused great trouble here, but neither you, nor Mrs Watson, is to blame for that – we do not choose our relatives. However, there is something else I want to speak to you about. I have just received the autopsy report of the dead companion of Lady Emily."

"Yes?" the doctor raised his fine eyebrows. "It seemed straightforward from what I heard from Dr Waters, down at the Convalescent Hospital."

"Not straightforward at all, sir. The deceased woman, Tanya

Illich, appears from the autopsy report to have committed *suicide*. It appears now, *not* to be murder, as we first thought."

"But I don't understand. She died from hydrogen cyanide poisoning didn't she?"

"Indeed she did, sir. However, the poison came from the locket, she was wearing around her neck. Believe it or not, she seems to have been wearing – for years possibly – a suicide capsule similar to the ones given to our secret service personnel, in time of war – in case they are caught and, through torture, reveal secret information."

"Good grief!" The famous doctor was startled. "How positively theatrical, and yet, how appropriate! That group of people consider themselves to be martyrs to the Cause, and so I suppose, from their point of view, it is totally logical.

"I would like, however, to know how they get their hands on such capsules!"

The doctor straightened his immaculate cuffs. "What you tell me, doesn't make sense. Why, in the world, would that woman want to commit suicide? She had a fool of an extremely wealthy woman, keeping her in a state of luxury that the poor woman had never experienced in her life; someone, who was equally ready to foot the bill for every idiotic pamphlet, and activity, the deceased woman engaged in. No, I'm sorry, murder makes more sense than that."

"Exactly my own thoughts, Doctor, but unfortunately I'm stuck with the facts."

Peters coughed a little apologetically. "Doctor, would you do me a favour? Would you please tell your aunt about the suicide? I really have had a terrible day and I don't want to have to face her again.

"However, that's a weak excuse and I'm wrong to even ask you to do that. If you have to dash off, don't worry, I'll do it, of course …"

"Say not another word, my very dear Inspector," the doctor replied getting wearily to his feet, "I understand perfectly. I'll just run up to her room on my way out and tell her. Then I'm hoping to spend a few minutes with dear Anne Watson …"

"Oh, dear, that reminds me; wait a minute!" interrupted Peters, "I clean forgot: Mrs Watson asked me to apologize for her not informing you of the death, of poor Harry Scott. She was fearfully upset with Billy nearly dying."

"No! I *was* informed about Harry's death, but not about Billy."

"Indeed, yes; both Mrs Watson and Billy thought the world of Dr Scott. They were fearfully upset by his suicide …"

"Brought about by my terrible aunt! Major Waters informed me about the death. Oh, dear Lord, Inspector, what are we to do with her?

"Do you know, the other day I happened to hear a Christian woman say that the more she is around children, the easier she finds it to believe in Original Sin," he laughed gently.

"I would like to add to that: The more I am around my Aunt Emily, the more I am convinced of the reality of evil!" Both men smiled, at the little joke, and the doctor continued:

"Yes, poor dear Harry Scott! He was a wonderful, gentle soul, Inspector. I knew him at University; a gentleman in every sense of the word, with a wonderful brain."

The doctor sighed. "Oh well, I must stop talking and get away. After I see Anne for a few minutes, I am needed at the big Military Hospital up at Wembly Park. Good bye, Inspector." The men shook hands hastily and Dr Gascoigne-Ridley hurried from the room.

Inspector Peters spent ten minutes gathering up his papers. It had been a long day and he was very tired. The autopsy report blows all our plans for tomorrow to smithereens, he reflected. Oh well, we'll deal with that tomorrow; I've had enough today.

He stood up. Through the window he could see the doctor's chauffeur waiting patiently in the big Rolls. He was aware of feet running down the stairs and the sound of the doctor's powerful car starting.

Ten minutes later, Peters left the room, and passing through the hall foyer, was surprised to hear Lady Emily speaking on the telephone installed there for the convenience of guests. She sounded furious.

"I have told you three times already! Are you an idiot, or something? I want them *tonight*! Not tomorrow! No, I will take no refusal! Well, send them by taxi! Cost is no object; charge what you want; I *must* have them … Listen to me, you nincompoop …"

Peters hastened his steps – he had no desire to be caught by Lady Emily so, hurriedly leaving the building, walked to the bus stop to begin the tedious journey home to his boarding house.

He usually thought of the place where he lodged as boringly and drearily commonplace, but now, it was beginning to appear sane, unpretentious, and comforting.

He longed just to be home, away from sudden death, foolish people and incomprehensible mysteries – and especially away from that dreadful woman, Emily!

CHAPTER 16

On Friday morning the policemen met again in the small parlour of the pub.

They had arrived early and had just heard the astonishing news of the autopsy report. They were staring at Inspector Peters, with unbelieving eyes. The silence was broken by Constable Potts.

"Crikey! If that doesn't take the bloomin' cake! *A suicide tablet!*"

Sergeant Pierce took the news as a personal insult. "It's disgraceful, that's what it is! The whole thing makes us look ridiculous! Who ever heard of somebody wearing a bloody time-bomb around their neck? That's what it was, a time-bomb!"

"Not exactly, Pierce, old chap," Peters soothed his sergeant. "You had to remove the capsule, bite on it to break it with your teeth; only then, was the poison released into the body."

Pierce was about to burst forth again, but young Constable Manders forestalled him: "Sir, did the doctor say how long it would take to work, once the woman had bitten on the capsule?"

"Yes, Constable, he did. I'm afraid, for once, the reality matches what we've all seen at the Pictures. It's all over in about one minute, with one of those tablets – they're designed for a very quick result – for obvious reasons."

"Pretty gruesome, sir," Manders observed, uneasily.

Pierce had rallied. "But, Inspector, is the doctor sure that's what happened? I mean, that it *was* suicide? Couldn't someone else have administered cyanide? Even I know, that the damn stuff is soluble in liquid."

"Theoretically, you're completely right, Pierce," conceded Peters, "but the composition of the suicide tablet is unique; the tests prove the cyanide in the corpse, is in the same, unique, combination. Therefore, it must have come from Tanya's locket and she always wore that around her neck. The doctor said he was prepared to swear that there were dust traces of the poison within the locket itself."

"Well, sir," said Potts, "thank the Lord we had this meeting before we started hauling in the suspects, for questioning. They'll all be here in a few minutes' time; we told them nine o'clock. We'd certainly look damn fools, if we had done that. So there's something to be pleased about."

"You're a sensible and practical man, Constable," Peters replied with a sigh. "Yet, I too feel cheated somehow, but that's ridiculous. I should – we *all* should – be glad it *is* suicide, for it means, there's not a killer out there we have to try to catch. Now, what I thought we'd do …" There was a sharp knock on the door, it opened, and Betty came in. She closed the door behind her and almost whispered to the men.

"Inspector, there's a Mr Bickerton, of Bickerton, Bickerton and Symthe who demands to see you immediately. They're that posh firm of solicitors, from Tavistock. The gentleman said to tell you that he represented Lady Emily …"

"Really? What the hell has she done now? Yes, of course Betty, thank you, I'll see him immediately." Betty surprised the men by remaining where she was, but now was smiling hugely.

"And, Inspector, he is accompanied by the lady herself. And …" Betty couldn't control herself any longer and begin to giggle, "just wait till you see her!" She hurried from the room with her apron to her mouth.

"What the bloody hell!" Peters exclaimed. "All right, chaps. Wait for me will you?" He left the room.

He found Betty outside the door. She led him silently to the land-lord's private office, where she had placed the visitors. She tapped on the door and announced the inspector.

Peters entered the room and stood quite still. There was an elderly man sitting at the table, with solicitor written all over him, while Lady Emily was standing near the window.

Emily was dressed in full, and extravagant, mourning, from her head to her feet. Her black mourning dress was mid-calf in length, with long sleeves and a high neck. The dress was very full, and beaded heavily in black jet – which matched the jet jewellery she wore at her neck and ears.

She wore black stockings and shoes and over her head and shoulders, she wore a long black, very beautiful, chiffon shawl, which she used to dab artistically at her eyes and lips, continually being careful, each time, never to actually touch her skin, so her makeup was kept safe.

The cherry lipstick she usually wore was replaced by a faint pink, and her eyes were heavy with mascara, giving her the look of a tragic stage actress.

Inspector Peters was highly diverted, but kept his face blank as he walked briskly to the front of the desk, and sat down. He looked at the solicitor.

"Good Morning Mr Bickerton, we have met before. Good morning, Lady Emily."

"Indeed we have, Inspector," quavered the elderly man, "I have told her Ladyship that she couldn't be in better hands than yours, sir, in this situation."

"That's very generous of you, sir," Peters replied. "Could you please tell me exactly what I can do for you; if it is within my power to do so, I shall be happy to oblige."

The solicitor shot a quick glance at his client, but she still stood mute at the window, her eyes averted. Seeing that he was going to get no help from her, he cleared his throat.

"Inspector, the Lady Emily has learned from her nephew, you have decided that Miss Illich's death, was not murder, but suicide. Is that correct?"

"Not exactly, Mr Bickerton," Peters qualified. "It is not my place to decide that – the Coroner will do that. However, from the results of the autopsy, it appears that the actual poison came from inside the locket that Miss Illich wore around her neck."

"Goodness gracious me!" the solicitor was clearly horrified by this piece of information.

"Exactly so, sir," Peters continued, "therefore, for that reason and for the fact that it appears that the locket, never left the neck of the deceased, it is hard to imagine any other conclusion to draw, except suicide. What would you think in my place?"

"Exactly as you have done, Inspector!

"But, my client, Inspector – whom we, as a firm, are privileged to serve – believes, that conclusion cannot be correct, as there was, in my client's opinion, absolutely no reason for the woman to commit suicide, but on the contrary, every reason to live."

"I'm afraid that is too vague for me to do anything with, Mr Bickerton. Unless Lady Emily is more forthcoming, in giving us any information she has, or thinks she has, then the verdict will undoubtedly be suicide."

Lady Emily forgot her tragic pose for a moment, and spoke sharply to her solicitor. "For goodness sake, you old idiot, show him the document immediately and get it over with!" She then re-membered her pose and pretended to take no more interest in the conversation. Mr Bickerton, on the other hand, was tremulous, as he fumbled with a thick document. He opened the stiff pages, and placed them in front of the Inspector.

Peters read swiftly, and his eyes opened wide in astonishment.

"Is it permissible, sir, to ask for a rough and ready estimate, of just what the entire estate is worth – that is, everything put together?"

"As you have now seen the Will, I don't see much point in not revealing other facts – unless my client thinks otherwise?" he shot a terrified glance at Lady Emily, who shook her head impatiently, "then, in that case, I would make a guess, a very rough guess, mind you: it would be in the region of half a million pounds."

"Good gracious! …Thank you, Mr Bickerton. Yes … I do understand why your client finds it hard to reconcile suicide with this document.

"I do have to ask a really pertinent question though of you, or your client: Did the deceased know of this document? I notice it is not signed."

Lady Emily detached herself from the wall and stood at the desk.

"Inspector Peters, after I had been to see Mr Bickerton the other day, I informed Tanya of what I had done and of all the details of the estate. She understood fully she was to be sole beneficiary. I told her I would be signing the Will as soon as it was drawn up, which we expected would be today."

"Lady Emily, please tell me truly: was Tanya delighted, or worried, or apprehensive, at this extraordinary news?"

"Inspector, she was absolutely thrilled; speechless with excitement, and gratitude." She dabbed again at her eyes and moved to the door. "That is all I can bear at the moment. Thank you, Mr Bickerton, for coming out here, this morning. I must go to rest now; I am not feeling well." Lady Emily made a gracious and beautiful exit from the room, a cloud of billowing black chiffon floating after her.

As soon as she had left the room, Mr Bickerton stood up. "Well, you can't choose your clients, Inspector – neither, unfortunately, can we! I had important meetings this morning which I had to cancel, so I must hurry off now. If you need any more information, please just phone me; there is absolutely no need to enquire of my client, for permission to do so." The old man gave a sly wink, shook hands, and began to gather his papers before he left the room.

Inspector Peters asked the elderly man a couple of questions which were answered briefly. After the solicitor left the room, Peters sat still for a moment. Well, who would believe it? It's becoming more like the bloody motion Pictures every minute. I can't wait to hear what Sergeant Pierce is going to say *to this*!

CHAPTER 17

In fact, Peters's news was received in dead silence. The three policemen stared at their superior as though he had gone mad. It was, however, Sergeant Pierce who first recovered.

"*Half a million* pounds! That's five hundred thousand pounds! No, it simply can't be! That's a sum that is impossible even to comprehend. Yes, I could understand a fabulous fortune of, say, fifty thousand pounds, but half a million!" His eyes were like saucers.

"That's what it is, chaps," assured the inspector. "I know it's a sum that even exceeds the imagination of the stuff we see on the screen at the Pictures."

Manders was shocked into seriousness by the actual amount. "Sir, do you think the solicitor has got it right? I mean, given the … er … eccentricities of the Lady Emily, I can imagine her making a will in Tanya's favour for, say a few thousands, but … her entire fortune?"

"I had a quiet word with Mr Bickerton – he's a good old man – before he left and he told me, on the quiet, that Lady Emily said her family would get nothing of her money; she was quite determined on that.

"She also had told him that the young woman, Tanya Illich, had given her a whole new life. According to the solicitor, Emily now 'had a purpose and a motive for living and she was determined that the Cause should not fail for lack of funds', if she should die.

"Interestingly *for us*, Mr Bickerton was convinced that Lady Emily was completely genuine, in *believing* that she was going to die; that someone was out to murder her."

Constable Potts cleared his throat. "I have to believe what you're telling us, sir, but, truly, to me the whole thing stinks. Something's wrong somewhere." The elderly Constable stood up. He looked enquiringly at the inspector. "Sir, you haven't forgotten, have you? We have all the suspects outside now. It's after nine o'clock, and that's the time we told them to be here."

Inspector Peters slammed his fist down on the table. "Bloody hell, Constable, you are right, as you always are! With all that's happened this morning, I forgot all about them." He stood, thinking rapidly.

"Look, chaps, we'll have to continue now, treating the case as if it were murder. In spite of the wretched cyanide in the locket, there is absolutely no motive whatsoever for Tanya taking her own life. We all said it didn't make sense; now we have *proof* that it doesn't. Now, about those outside …

"Manders, go out with Constable Potts, and arrange the people in the order in which they came to the pub to see Lady Emily. We should be able to eliminate the early ones if they are telling the truth. Pierce, you remain here with me." Peters looked at Constable Potts.

"Potts, we don't really know where we are on this one. Would you do your 'grandfather' act out there with the people; introduce Manders to them, if they don't already know him … and both of you – you know – just chat with them; see what you can discover, especially try to discover, in general conversation, whether they can actually substantiate each other's alibi."

He noticed the look on Potts' face. "I know, Potts, believe me, I do. They are not only your friends, they are ours as well, but we've got to do our duty. Understood?"

"You're totally right, sir. You can't have it both ways in our job, can you? Come along Manders, let's see what we can find out – you can concentrate on the young couple, I'll do the oldies."

There was another sharp knock on the door. Mr Jones came in. "Excuse me, Inspector Peters: there's another urgent call for you. Look, I think it would be easier for you to use my office – as you did last summer when you were here. The telephone and the typewriter are there. Would that be easier for you?"

"You are such a practical man, Mr Jones," Peters replied. "Yes, it would be wonderful. Thank you for your generosity. We'll move in there now; I'll take the call there." He looked at Pierce. "Sergeant, bring all the notes and books into the office; I'll answer the call now."

In Mr Jones' office, Peters was surprised to hear the voice of the solicitor, Mr McKenzie senior, on the phone.

"This is a surprise, sir. I didn't expect the call to be from you."

"As a matter of fact, Inspector, I feel rather embarrassed about it all."

"What exactly is the matter? If it is about your wife being here to answer a few questions – I believe she is here, I haven't seen her yet – you can rest assured …"

"No, it's nothing to do with Harriet. I can hardly see you giving her the Third Degree – the only thing Harriet is capable of killing are snails; she's quite ruthless with them!" The solicitor laughed.

"Well, that's a relief anyhow," Peters chuckled, "but, please go ahead and just tell me what the matter is …"

"It's about Bert Liveridge …"

"No! Don't tell me he has gone to you for legal assistance!"

"He has, Inspector. He came to me professionally, to get my advice. I have assured him that, if what he says is actually *true*, it would be slanderous if the person were still alive, but as she is dead, he cannot be legally guilty of slander, but regarding conspiracy to murder, that's another question altogether."

"But I don't understand."

"You see, Inspector, he claims that the deceased, Tanya Illich, came to him while he was at the pub on Thursday night and …wait for it … asked him – for the good of the Cause – if he would kill Lady Emily."

"WHAT?" Peters actually shouted, alarming Pierce, who had just entered the room.

"Yes, I was as shocked as you are. I informed him I was going to report the conversation to you, but if he wanted me to act for him in any further capacity, he would have to get another solicitor."

"Thank you, Mr McKenzie for your information. Could I ask a favour of you – it's an awful cheek?"

"Ask away, Inspector, we are heavily in your debt, in this village, for what you have done for us since you came here."

"That's very nice of you, sir. Well, I'm out of my depth here, legally. May I ask if Bert Liveridge agreed to Tanya's request?"

"According to him, he didn't, but was so shocked at the sum he was to receive – it was ten thousands pounds, believe it or not – that he was dumbfounded. Miss Illich went off, telling him to think it over and let her know this morning, at the pub."

"So, can we say that he entered into a conspiracy to murder, even if it was only tacit consent?"

"This is where it gets tricky. I had to look it up myself. According to the Law books, the consensus of opinion is that a charge of conspiracy to murder, can only be upheld, if you can establish that the conspirators believed that it was *possible* to commit the murder.

"I think, Inspector, it might be possible to charge him with that, but the problem is, firstly: we have only his word that any of this is even true, and secondly, the murder is certainly not *possible* to commit *now*, with the main conspirator, who had the money, dead.

"Apparently the Illich woman told Liveridge she would inherit all of Lady Emily's money. It would have been possible to pursue the charge while Tanya was alive, but not now she's dead. It's my belief that the charge wouldn't stick; it would be thrown out, and we'd be accused of wasting the time of the court, if we proceeded."

"I see."

"That was the reason I rang you. I would never otherwise breach client confidentiality. I think, Inspector that it's just a silly old chap who was knocked sideways by the offer of a huge amount of money, then came to his senses, and wanted desperately to distance himself, from the whole affair.

"You see, I've known old Bert a long time – in many ways just a silly old bugger, but very shrewd. That's the reason he came to me. I have no evidence for this, but I think someone else knows of this offer, made to Bert.

"It smells a bit, him suddenly being so anxious 'to help the police with their enquiries' – that is out of character. Perhaps I'm just getting cynical in my old age. Anyhow, that's the story, Inspector."

"Thank you again, Mr McKenzie. You have been extremely helpful. I'll send a constable right away for Mr Liveridge. Good grief, this case is the weirdest I've ever had; more and more, like something you see at the cinema."

"I agree, Inspector. Well, when Harriet comes in for the grilling, tell her I told you she was capable of the most dreadful crimes; that young George and I live in perpetual dread of her and are thinking of employing a taster for our food."

The solicitor laughed heartily. "Good bye, Inspector, you lead an exciting life!" He cut the connection.

Peters stood staring into space with the receiver in his hand. He spun round and saw the Sergeant. "Pierce, go out immediately and bring in Manders." Peters sat down at the desk. Within a minute, Manders was standing before him.

"Constable, take a car and go and pick up Bert Liveridge. Take no refusal; he must come here. If he protests, tell him he will be arrested and placed in a cell at the police station at Tavistock. Understood?"

"Yes, sir," Manders answered. "Do I answer any of his questions, sir?"

"No. We'll keep him in suspense, as long as we can; we might get the truth out of him if he's scared enough. Off you go, now." Manders left and Peters turned to Pierce. "Get an ear-full of this, Pierce. Truly this case gets more and more ridiculous by the minute."

Pierce was suitably impressed by the absurdity of the whole situation and expressed himself fairly luridly, but was interrupted by Constable Potts bringing in the first of the 'suspects'. Both men stood as Harriet McKenzie came into the room.

She knew both of the men, and shook hands with them.

"I never dreamt I would be giving evidence in a murder case, Inspector," she began, "but if I have any information that you need, just go ahead and ask me anything."

"We can only hope that every other person feels the same as you do, Mrs McKenzie," Peters assured her and started to smile. "I have to tell you: your husband was just on the phone to me – no, not about you being here, this morning – but he warned me to be on the lookout, as you were, without doubt, the killer."

Harriet started to laugh and both men joined in. She had been nervous and tense, when she had come into the room, but now felt relaxed with these men, whom she knew so well.

"I suspect, Mrs McKenzie," Peters smiled, "you are longing to get back to your lovely garden where a dozen things need doing now that winter has begun, so I'll not keep you long. Just tell me a couple of things, Mrs McKenzie," Peters said. "Can I ask you for an honest answer to this: did you like the deceased woman?"

Harriet settled herself more comfortably in her chair, and cradled her chin in her hand. "Honestly? No, I didn't. I was appalled by what she believed and what she was actually doing in our country, especially as we are battling to survive in this war, as it is."

"Thank you. Now, did Tanya Illich come to your house?"

"Twice, Inspector. The first time she introduced herself as a close friend of Lady Emily, and as I had met that woman the day before, I took her in and intended to offer her tea." Harriet's plump and pleasant middle-aged face began to flush.

"It only took a couple of minutes for me to learn, what she was doing in our village. I was so outraged, I stood up and asked her to leave my house, which she did."

"But she came again?"

"She did. I was surprised at that. I opened the door, said I was not interested, and closed the door in her face. That's the sum total of my involvement with that woman."

"Apart from her doctrines, what did you think of her?"

"I thought she was a decent, well-brought up girl, and I was intensely sorry for her. I thought she had been 'got at' by the Reds and they had brainwashed her completely. There's no doubt in my mind she believed wholeheartedly in what she was preaching."

"Now about yesterday morning; why were you coming to see Lady Emily?"

'She actually rang and asked me to come. I couldn't understand why, but I grabbed the chance of speaking to her. I had become incensed at what that woman had done to a number of innocent people.

"I cannot pretend that I wasn't mainly angry that she had ruined the relationship between my son and Annie Watson's daughter, Penelope. They were engaged, and both families were so looking forward to the marriage, then within one day of meeting Penelope, Lady Emily had managed to break the engagement."

"I can easily understand your reaction. But what did you hope to achieve coming here to see the woman?"

"Achieve? I don't honestly know. I think I basically wanted to let off steam. I think it was the death of that very nice sick soldier, Dr Scott, which was the final straw. His death and the effect on the poor Watson boy – really it was infamous!" Harriet's voice trembled with indignation.

"And, when you got here … incidentally, *when* did you get here?"

"It was just striking nine when I entered the foyer."

"Good, note that Pierce. Right, Mrs McKenzie, did you speak to Lady Emily?"

"Yes, I met Betty in the foyer – she was doing some housework there – and I asked for Lady Emily and she directed me to the bar room. I found the lady sitting in the window alcove seat."

"And?"

Harriet McKenzie flushed scarlet. "I made a fool of myself, Inspector, that's what I did. I told that woman what I thought of her and her wicked interference … and … she …" Harriet paused.

"Yes?"

"She just laughed! She *laughed* at me, and *dismissed* me like a servant! She went to the bar and rang the bell.

"Betty came in, and that woman asked for a glass and a small bottle of soda water. Betty served her and Lady Emily went back to her seat, ignoring me. I was left standing, feeling more foolish than I have ever felt in my life.

"I realised I should never have come. Trying to gather up some shreds of dignity, I bade her good morning, and left." Harriet looked at the Inspector shrewdly, "and before you ask me, I was with her for exactly ten minutes; it was ten minutes past nine when I left the inn."

"Thank you Mrs McKenzie, a very lucid and exact account. Believe me, I do understand how painful the interview would have been, with that particular woman.

"Go home and work in your beautiful garden, slaughter a number of snails, without mercy and try to forget about this situation." Peters stood up. "Pierce!"

The sergeant stood up and opened the door for Harriet. As soon as Potts saw Mrs McKenzie leave, he brought Mrs Hennessy to the office.

Laura was relieved to see that Harriet came from the interview, smiling; obviously it was not going to be too difficult. Inspector

Peters made a point of settling her comfortably in her chair and asking about her daughter, Joan.

"That's the problem, Inspector; that's how I got into this mess."

"Yes?"

"Well, you see, Lady Emily spread rumours about my daughter flirting with soldiers at the Red Cross Hospital – she's a VAD – and Dan Kelly was furious. It seems they have now broken off their understanding."

"Goodness me! Do you think they will make it up? I mean, it doesn't sound very serious does it, even if it were true. What is Dan thinking of? Joan's a fine girl."

"She is that, Inspector and I was happy about the idea of her marrying Dan. He's a good, steady hard-working young man. There's the difference in religion, of course, but that didn't seem to worry Hannah Kelly and it didn't worry me.

"The Kellys are a highly respected family here. I think I've known the family all of Dan's life. There was something comforting about the idea of my Joan marrying a man, you've always known, isn't there?"

"Yes, there is. I can imagine most mothers saying the same thing. So you came here yesterday to admonish Lady Emily, for her tale-bearing, is that it?"

"Well she rang, and asked to see me; I was surprised at that. However, I decided I would go, and I did. I came just after Mrs McKenzie. She was coming out of the hotel as I entered …"

"So that'd be about a quarter past nine?"

Laura looked surprised. "Yes, about that."

"And what happened?"

"Well, I found that woman. She was seated in the window seat. She had a drink of something on the table; I don't think she had started to drink it.

"I felt nervous and silly and once I got to the table, I found it almost impossible to say anything at all! I was mortified. I stood there, like a country-bumpkin and ... *that* woman ... she insulted me!" Poor Laura's face flamed red.

Peters asked gently, "Mrs Hennessy, would you please tell me what exactly that woman said to you?" Laura swallowed, and replied:

"She said: 'I am not a teacher of the dumb. Go away; this is not my morning for entertaining idiots!'"

"That is a terrible thing to say, Mrs Hennessy. I feel for you. What did you do?"

"I stumbled out of the place, as quickly as I could; vowing that I would never get myself into such a situation ever again. I felt as if I could have killed ... Oh, my God, what have I said?" Tears started to form in the middle-aged eyes. Laura looked distraught.

"Please, Mrs Hennessy, do stop. You'll make yourself ill. You have said nothing wrong; – we all say things like that. It means nothing, believe me. You had a terrible, embarrassing, and upsetting experience. I feel extremely sorry you had to undergo that."

Peters stood up. "Mrs Hennessy, Sergeant Pierce will see you out. Thank you for coming and for your courtesy." Laura hurried from the room.

The door opened and Constable Manders put his head in. "Inspector, I have Bert Liveridge; I've put him in the parlour, Constable Potts is guarding him. What do you want done with him?"

"Bring Sergeant Pierce back to me Manders."

When Pierce came hurrying in, Peters gave new orders.

"Pierce, I want you to take over the questioning, while I deal with Bert Liveridge. I'll use Manders to take notes; you bring Potts here, to do the same for you. OK?"

"Right, sir, I think the next ones are Dan and Bianca. Do you want me to see them together, or separately?"

"No, together. They've been sitting there together, and most probably came here together, so whether their story is true, or false, it'll be the same for each of them. But, Pierce, lad, make sure you note the times and don't forget the poison glass, on the table."

"Understood, sir."

Peters hurried from the office room, to the small parlour where he found a querulous Bert Liveridge and Constable Potts looking harassed.

"Constable Potts please go to Sergeant Pierce. He needs you for the interviews. Manders will be helping me." Potts hurried away; Manders came in, and sat unobtrusively near the window, taking out his notebook.

Peters sat and looked at the small man opposite him. Bert went to speak, but Peters held up his hand. The silence lengthened.

"I've had a phone call from Mr McKenzie, Mr Liveridge."

"So?"

"For your own sake, Mr Liveridge, I would advise you to keep a civil tongue in your head. There is a fearful charge of being an accessory to murder hanging over you at this moment."

"*Strewth*! Who said anything about a charge? Mr McKenzie said if I told you the truth, I am actually guilty of nothing …"

"In relation to *slander*, that is true. The other charge of entering into a *conspiracy to murder* is still wide open.

"I think it is in your own interests, Mr Liveridge, to tell me the truth, and that means the *whole truth* about the affair. Even then, it's only taking your word for it. You have no proof that you did not intend to carry out the operation.

"I have to tell you that, regardless of what you tell me now, I can make no promises of what will happen – we are talking here of a criminal offence."

Bert attempted to speak; again Peters held up his hand. "However, if you fully, and completely tell me, all you know of the situation and if you convince me that you are telling the truth, then naturally that alters the case. I will then do the best I can for you."

"I *am* telling the truth – that's God's truth."

"That's hardly convincing, Mr Liveridge, coming from an atheist!

Look, why don't you simply tell me all about the whole affair." Peters' voice softened; became less official.

"Try to be a sensible chap, Mr Liveridge. You have got yourself into a dreadful mess, which does not leave me much room to manoeuvre."

"All right, all right, I will. It was like this. On Thursday night, I was in the pub having a drink with my next door neighbour, old Alf Cookson. I don't usually like sitting with him, as he has kidney trouble; he's off to the lavatory every few minutes.

"Well, on one of his visits to the lav, Tanya came into the bar, and seeing me, came over thinking I was alone. She asked if I would come outside for a moment, as she had something very important to tell me.

"She sounded very excited. I knew that Alf would be a good while in the lavatory, so I went with Tanya out of the building and we walked round the back of the pub in the dark, where it was private."

"What happened then?"

"I got the shock of my life. That's what! Tanya asked me how much money I would need to really set me up for the rest of my life. I thought she was joking.

"I said, as a joke, 'Oh, about ten thousand pounds would do' and, blow me down flat, if she didn't say, 'Well, let's take that as the amount for the job then, shall we?'

"I didn't know what the hell she was talking about, so I asked: 'What job?' and she took the wind out of my sails by saying calmly: 'I want you to kill Lady Emily for me'.

"I asked her if she was joking; she tells me she'd never been more serious. She also told me, that if I was a really convinced communist, as I'd said I was, then I'd have no hesitation in doing what she asked, as it would be the means of furthering the Cause in Australia – more than ever had been possible, before."

"Didn't you wonder where the money was to come from?"

"Course I did, I'm not stupid!" Bert snapped angrily. "I asked her, didn't I?

"She said that Lady Emily was leaving her fortune to her and once the woman was dead, Tanya would have the entire fortune for herself – she would be one of the richest women in Australia."

"And you agreed to do this?"

"Not on your bloody life, I didn't! Don't you go putting words into my mouth!

"I was fair dumbfounded, I was. I couldn't think of anything to say. I never, in all my life, have had *one* thousand pounds, let alone *ten*.

"I was gasping at the thought of what I could do with that amount of money; I really didn't think about the job I was being asked to do at all.

"Tanya saw I was confused, she told me, very kindly, to leave it for the moment; to think on it overnight, and to see her in the morning at the pub – to let her know my decision.

"And that's what I did. We parted then; she went back upstairs, and I joined Alf in the bar."

"Mr Liveridge, did Tanya indicate the method to use in the murder of Lady Emily?"

"Yes, she did. She told me that the rich dame made a habit of taking a short walk in the blackout, each evening, before going to bed – usually just around the outside of the pub.

"She did this to provoke old Mr Jones, who had tried to tell her that this was a very dangerous thing to do in the blackout – she could get bashed with so many soldiers about – which was true.

"Anyhow, Tanya thought it would be easy to hit the woman with an iron bar, or something, and no one would ever know who did it."

"And, how would you both be safe from suspicion?"

"She had that worked out as well. She would come into the bar, and ask me – in front of everyone-to come up to her sitting room to discuss our plans for spreading the Word; once there, I would slip out down the back stairs, while she would keep talking, as though I was in the room – in case anyone was listening.

Peters' face was a picture of outrage as he stared at Liveridge.

"Mr Liveridge, I am simply appalled at what I am hearing. By your own words you confess that you calmly listened to a plan to murder a defenceless woman, then ask me to believe that you did not intend to do it?"

Bert Liveridge began to sweat. "I've told you the whole truth. Earlier today you asked me why I just sat there in the corner of the bar room and didn't speak to Tanya. I was bloody terrified, that's why.

"When I saw her dead, I knew I had no chance anymore of telling her I wouldn't kill the other one. I kept thinking I had done it; that I had killed *Tanya* somehow, I was so confused!"

Manders caught Inspector Peters' eye. "Yes, Constable?" he asked.

"May I ask a question, sir?"

"No, you mayn't," shouted Bert, "you're just a baby copper you are, so you keep your place and continue with your scribbling." He turned to Peters. "He man-handled me, he did, you know, in the car – I think I might charge him."

"Just as well for you that I did grab you, you silly chap," Manders rejoined sharply. Turning to Peters he explained. "Just after we had set off, sir, Mr Liveridge attempted to leap from the car. I was only able to grab him in time to save his worthless life."

"I see. Next time, Constable Manders, please don't bother; it's not worth saving. Well, I can guess, Mr Liveridge, what the constable was going to ask you, for it intrigues me as well.

"*Why* are you telling me all this. If you had kept quiet, I wouldn't have even known about it. As it is, you've put yourself in a very equivocal position with the law. Could it have been that someone overheard you talking with Tanya Illich?"

"Blimey, how could you have known that?"

"Bert," the Inspector said gently, "I think you've been a fool. Let's have it; the truth now ..."

Bert Liveridge took out a non-too-clean handkerchief and mopped his face and neck.

"Well, apparently my blooming neighbour, Alf, overheard us from the lavatory. He said our voices could be plainly heard through the window.

"Thankfully, he was the only one in the lav at the time. Anyhow, he heard it all, and was on to me as soon as I returned to the bar.

"He's very much in with the Presbyterian Minister, Mr Norman – goes to church every Sunday and all that – he said he was going to tell Mr Norman what he heard; that if I didn't come and tell you about it, it would be his duty to go to the police.

"His *duty*! The silly old bugger knows that I wouldn't kill anyone. I even feel sick having to put a rabbit down.

"That's the truth of the whole matter and I was here this morning simply to see Tanya to tell her it was 'not on' – I wasn't putting my head in the noose for any Cause, whether it be hers, or anyone else's."

"So, when you turned up here and found Tanya dead, what happened then?"

"I didn't know what to do. I went home and spoke to Alf; he said if I didn't come straight away to the police, he would. I thought I'd get a bit of advice first, so I called on Mr McKenzie and he advised me to come to you immediately.

"I was just getting ready to come here, when that burly, muscle-bound, baby-policeman, hauled me off like a bag of potatoes."

Peters sighed windily.

"Before I finish with you, Mr Liveridge, you'll wish you were a bag of potatoes!

"Now, I have another very important question to put to you – your whole future could depend on it. Tell me this, honestly, – your whole freedom depends on it: What was in the locket around Tanya's neck?"

Bert Liveridge's eyes goggled; his face a mask of incomprehension as he stared at the Inspector: "What do you mean? What bloody locket … Oh, do you mean that gold thing … around her neck?

"How the bloody hell should I know? Most probably a tiny picture of some bloke – that's what's usually there, isn't it? It was just some bit of fancy junk women wear, wasn't it?

"I'm not interested in women's jewellery – as apparently, some policemen are."

"Right!" Peters stood up. "You're a damn nuisance, Liveridge, and a waste of my time, but I've got to deal with you.

"You will consider yourself under arrest and remain in this room; leave it for one moment unaccompanied by a policeman and you will be taken, under arrest, to Tavistock Police Station and placed in a cell.

"You are detained until I have interviewed Mr Cookson. I shall then decide whether to proceed further, and charge you. You've admitted that you participated in a conversation about a conspiracy to murder. I have no option but to investigate this thoroughly.

"I think you've just been a silly clown, but unfortunately, you have no witnesses to substantiate your decision not to proceed, with the murder. I have to tell you that you can have a solicitor present, if you so wish."

Bert Liveridge looked stricken and feebly waved away the offer of a solicitor. He promised not to leave the room in the pub. He was given permission to smoke, if he wished.

Inspector Peters then sent Manders to collect Alf Cookson, and only then was able to re-join Pierce in the office. He was just in time to see Dan Kelly and Bianca leave the room.

Peters smiled at the couple; Dan greeted him cheerfully, but Bianca looked at him coldly.

"What can you tell me, Pierce?" Sergeant Pierce gathered his notes together.

"Seems pretty straight forward, sir. They arrived together at a quarter to ten o'clock, went straight to the bar; they could see Lady Emily, from outside, sitting at the window.

"Dan had his say and was not very convincing about how upset he was about the break-up with Joan Hennessy, but it was Bianca who really took on Lady Emily; called her some dreadful words in Italian – so she told me – and ended the tirade, by spitting at the astonished lady."

"And the drink and the time they left?"

"The glass of soda water was half empty and Lady Emily actually drank some while they were there – at least they say she did – and they left the inn at five minutes to ten, got into their buggy and drove home.

"They'd only been home a little over an hour, when they were informed by Betty, that there'd been a murder at the pub. They thought the victim was Lady Emily and returned to the pub. That's all, sir."

Peters informed the two policemen of what had occurred with Bert Liveridge and then Potts brought in the next person to be interviewed, Thelma Kemp, the local doctor's wife. The elderly constable then went to the parlour to keep an eye on Bert Liveridge.

The Inspector greeted Mrs Kemp whom they knew well. She was flushed, and still angry at the memory of her visit to Lady Emily. Peters noticed that Thelma Kemp was not only angry, but embarrassed, as well. He sought to put her at ease by speaking of her husband.

"And how is your good man, Dr Kemp? Still frightfully busy as usual?"

Thelma sighed. "Just as busy, Inspector. Since the beginning of the war, with the desperate shortage of doctors for civilians, he's been run off his feet. He often says if another woman dares to give birth in the early hours of the morning, he'll run away to join the army!" She laughed.

"But it must be a great help to him, Mrs Kemp, with you being a qualified nursing sister yourself? That must remove a great deal of the time-consuming tasks from his shoulders."

"Well, I think it does. It leaves Edward free to concentrate on the difficult jobs. I handle all the paper work, and look after the wretched telephone with the endless calls. Also," she added darkly, "send out the bills!"

"Surely the people appreciate the incredible work the doctor is doing, and how overworked he is!" exclaimed Peters.

"Oh, yes. They're very *appreciative*. I only wish they'd show their appreciation by paying their bills. They seem to think it's only the third time the bill is sent out, that they have to think about actually paying it."

Thelma smiled, then became serious again. "But … this war! Inspector, do you think it will ever end?"

"It has to one day, Mrs Kemp, and until then, we have to keep pushing on the best we can. In our own job, cases such as this drive me mad, with frustration. As if we didn't have enough things to face, to have a foolish woman …"

"No, Inspector," contradicted Thelma, "not just a foolish woman, an *evil* woman – that's what I think she is. I'm the foolish one being silly enough to obey her call to come and see her yesterday."

"Why silly?"

"I was a complete fool, gentlemen, to have gone to see that dreadful woman at all. I don't know what possessed me to do so.

"No, that's not true, I do know. It was the death of my two dearest neighbours – the innocent, and very elderly, Mr and Mrs Nicholls. They've been my neighbours ever since Edward married me and brought me to this beautiful place, to live. They were always *there* … you know what I mean."

Tears trickled down Thelma's nose. "There! I'm making a fool of myself, but I loved the old couple, dearly. My own parents were killed when I was very young and the Nicholls were like parents to me. I miss them dearly. And, it's all through the machinations, of that evil woman."

Inspector Peters took Thelma's hand. "Mrs Kemp, please calm yourself. We do truly understand your grief and your indignation. Just a couple of simple questions and then you can get home to your good husband. Now, can you tell me at what time did you arrive at the pub yesterday morning?"

"I looked at the clock in the foyer, Inspector, it was just striking ten o'clock."

"Did you go straight into the bar?"

"Betty was in the passageway, from the kitchen, going to the bar and she told me that Lady Emily was seated there. I followed Betty into the bar, and just then, Tanya Illich came from the alcove where Lady Emily was sitting."

"*What*? Tanya was there at ten o'clock? What was she doing?" Mrs Kemp looked surprised at the question.

"Inspector, she was putting an empty bottle back on the bar, and ordered a gin and a small bottle of tonic water for Lady Emily. I waited until she had given these to the Lady, and when she left the room, I went across to speak to the Emily woman." Her face flushed red.

"And she was rude to you?"

"Rude? She was disgusting! Moreover, she was more than I could cope with. I was no match for her tongue. She told me exactly how low-born I was; how she knew I had thrown myself at my husband; that I was unable to have children for a very good reason which she intended to make public ... need I go on?"

"No, indeed, Mrs Kemp," Peters answered quickly. "Truly, all this is simply infamous. To me it is a miracle Lady Emily wasn't murdered years ago. I think she needed one of those husbands you read about, who beat their wives regularly once a week, for the good of their souls."

This was so ridiculous that Thelma began to smile, and her sense of shame began to fade.

"Oh, you are a good man, Inspector!" she exclaimed. "I've been a fool, and hopefully this will teach me a lesson. Any more questions?"

"Only one: did you notice the time, when you left, or any other person coming in after you."

"That's two questions, and the answer is yes, and yes. The time was ten minutes past ten, and Major Tim Johnson was coming into the foyer of the pub, just as I was leaving it."

Sergeant Pierce carefully wrote down the times. Peters rose, thanked Mrs Kemp and showed her out. Potts already had Tim Johnson ready to come in.

The policemen greeted the Major and were both delighted to see that he looked so well and strong again. Peters thought he would never forget his first meeting with this soldier, in the locked ward at that dreadful Army Mental Hospital, which now, thank goodness, was the splendid Convalescent Hospital. It seemed a miracle to look at him now, the picture of health.

"Yes, I'm fine again, thank you," Tim Johnson smiled at the men. "I'm still at the hospital, but am only on very mild medication now – practically nothing at all. It looks as if I will be transferred within the next week or two – my 'swinging the lead' is over," he laughed.

"Now about this wretched affair, Tim," Peters said, "Betty has mentioned that you spoke to Tanya on another occasion. Would you tell us about that?"

"I suppose it was a silly idea, but I was pretty upset about the death of Harry Scott. I knew him at Uni. He was a great bloke and Betty liked him too. We were talking about it – Betty and I – and she said something about some way of getting rid of the pair of them – Lady Emily and Tanya.

"I thought about it and decided to try a little bit of – not too subtle – 'divide and conquer' technique. I pretended to Tanya that I was a convert, but warned her that her association with the fabulously wealthy Lady Emily, was actually harming her chances here."

"What did you think of her, Tim?"

"Tanya? I'd never spoken to her before and I was very surprised to find her a decent and intelligent young woman, who believed totally, and implicitly, in what she taught." Tim smiled ruefully. "At Uni we were always sprouting Socialist rubbish, but then it was all a joke – something you did that was outrageous.

"I had never met an intelligent, dedicated communist before in my life. I have to admit I was impressed – not with her doctrines – they were treasonable in time of war – but with her sincerity."

"And, your reason for being here, yesterday morning?"

'Lady Emily had sent for me; I can't think why. Perhaps Tanya had spoken of me to her. Anyhow I decided to see if my 'divide and conquer' technique would work on Lady Emily; it had certainly impressed Tanya – or, so I believed – but I had no illusions the same technique would work with the Lady – she was a different kettle of fish.

"I was thinking up an approach when it all came to nothing."

"Oh, and why was that?"

"For the simple reason that when I came into the bar room, from the foyer, it was empty; not even Betty was there. I went out to the kitchen and asked where Betty was, and Mrs Jones told me she was upstairs. I asked where Lady Emily was, and was told she was in the bar, but she wasn't."

"So you didn't actually talk to Lady Emily at all?"

"That's right. I glimpsed Betty at the top of the stairs, as I was leaving then went back to the hospital … and, to forestall the next question: yes, I did note the time, it was half past ten o'clock."

"One last question, Tim: while you were at the table Lady Emily had been using, did you see a glass on the table?"

"I didn't go over to the table. I could see that there was no-one there from the doorway. I vaguely remember seeing something on the table … But no, I'm not sure I even saw that. It's a fair way from the actual bar to that table and the table's hidden a bit, by those palms.

"No, sorry, can't help there."

"Not to worry, Tim. I think you most probably saw Miss Amelia Tatley coming in, as you left didn't you?"

"Ah! I see why you are a detective, Inspector! Yes, I did. She's a fine old lady isn't she?"

"Indeed she is. Thank you Major, that is all. We both wish you well in your new posting. A pity really, I was kind of hoping, that you might be staying here."

"To be truthful, so was I, Inspector. There's a wonderful girl that I'd like to marry if she'd have me, but I haven't got up courage yet to ask her yet."

Peters laughed. "I wouldn't leave it too late, Tim, if I were you; Betty's a wonderful girl." Tim looked startled, blushed, then started to grin. He shook hands with the policemen and left the room.

Pierce looked very troubled. "It looks bad now doesn't it, sir? I've always admired the old lady."

"Yes, lad, I'm sorry, but it does. Ah well! Sometimes I hate my job." The door opened. "Yes, that's right, Miss Tatley, come in and sit down. Thank you Constable; you can go."

CHAPTER 18

Miss Tatley advanced to the inspector and shook his hand, then turned to the sergeant. 'It is a pleasure to meet you again, gentlemen, I remember vividly our last meeting. What a terrible time that was, wasn't it?"

"Thanks be to God, Miss Tatley, it all came right in the end."

"Yes … but, not before those two poor young men were murdered! Did you know, gentlemen, Mrs Loretta Corbett still comes to visit me, to talk about her son? I treasure her visits."

"I'm so glad of that, my dear Miss Tatley; I'm so grateful that you were there when you were so desperately needed." Peters pulled out a chair. "Please sit down; I'm sorry you have had a long wait."

"That is irrelevant, Inspector. You are serving the cause of Justice – my inconvenience is of no importance." Peters moved back to his own side of the desk.

"Now," he continued, "I believe you arrived here at the inn, to see Lady Emily, at about half past ten yesterday morning?"

"Yes, she sent a message to me by one of the Quarry boys that she wanted to see me. That surprised me. Yes, it must have been about half past ten, for I saw that nice gentleman, Major Johnson, leaving as I arrived."

"And you went straight into the bar room?"

"Well, I had to have a little look around first; I have never been in the bar room before. The room was empty. I was just coming out to ask Betty where Lady Emily was, when the woman herself walked in. She had come from the passageway at the other end of the bar – I believe that leads to the outside."

Peters looked up surprised. "Did she indeed? Where did she go?"

"Lady Emily went to her seat in the window alcove. She took up her glass, and put it down again, without tasting it, then, when I reached her table, she looked at me from head to toe, slowly and scornfully." Amelia's face flushed.

"Gentlemen, I don't think anyone has ever looked at me like that before in my life. It sounds ridiculous, but it was the most insulting, and humiliating, experience I've ever had – and all she did, was *look* at me."

"Who spoke first?"

"I think I did; I told her to behave like the lady she was supposed to be; that her behaviour was that of a trollop." Amelia blushed again. "I'm sorry to tell you I did say that". Amelia lowered her voice. "Between you and me, to be strictly honest, I don't actually *know* how a trollop does behave."

Peters and Pierce both laughed. Amelia looked surprised, and then smiled.

"Yes, I suppose that sounded ridiculous. Anyhow, as Lady Emily seemed determined not to speak, I spoke at length. I told her of the suffering she has caused; of the death of poor Dr Scott, then the near-death of my dear young friend, Billy Watson."

"Did Lady Emily seem impressed, or remorseful, to you?"

"Indeed, the exact opposite. She just sat there with that superior, silly, smile on her lips. I wanted to slap her face – isn't that a terrible thing? I wanted to slap her, as though she were a cheeky insolent brat – which is what I think she is."

"It most probably would have done her good. Tell me, Miss Tatley, did she speak at all?"

"Only at the end. I had run out of steam and was just about to walk away when she spoke softly …" Amelia's voice faltered.

"Would you please tell me, Miss Tatley, what Lady Emily said?"

Amelia Tatley blushed scarlet, but held her head high, staring at the opposite wall.

"She said she did not speak to despicable people – who had a criminal record!"

"Good grief! Will you tell us if that is true – impossible, as it sounds – Miss Tatley?"

"Yes, it is correct. No," the elderly woman held up her hand, "I'm sorry gentlemen, I cannot tell you what it was. I have decided to sell my little cottage, and leave the district. I could not live with my wonderful neighbours who have been my friends now for decades, when they get to know about me."

"But, my dear Miss Tatley, why need they ever know? Every secret is safe with Sergeant Pierce and with me, unless it has a bearing on a crime. Please reconsider, I beg of you. Annie Watson, I know, would be broken-hearted if you were to go away.

"Whatever it was, it can't have been very bad; you've had a long and distinguished career as a school teacher. Dear God help us! If anyone can say that they didn't do something sinful, or wrong, or even criminal, in their youth, they are simply telling lies."

Peters stood up, and went to Amelia's side of the table. She was now weeping openly. Peters gazed down on her long grey plaits which were wound round her head, which was now held in her hands. He put his hand gently on her shoulders.

"Miss Tatley, would you please tell me one more thing? That glass of drink you noticed on the table. Was it a clear liquid, can you remember?"

Amelia lifted her tear-streaked face. "I honestly cannot remember. I was looking at her face all the time. She was gathering her things together, as though she was about to leave – her purse and a magazine, I think. It was only when she was ready to leave that she did look up and speak to me.

"I was so shocked, I turned and rushed out of the building. I just wanted to get home as quickly as I could; I wanted to hide my face in shame. I should never have gone to the dreadful woman." She stood up.

"I'm sorry, I can't bear anymore. Please excuse me, gentlemen." She was weeping again, and hurried from the room, leaving behind her the two men sitting in an awkward silence.

Peters spoke first. "Well, that was bloody painful, lad. The poor old lady! What on earth could she have done? But, Pierce, do you realise what she has said? She has given us the *time* when Lady Emily left the table.

"Tanya must have come in almost immediately, after Miss Tatley left, and drank the liquid, still in the glass. There isn't time for anyone else. So, one of those we have seen – who came *after* ten o'clock – *must* have poisoned the glass – how, God alone knows – as Stephen Armitage is the only one left.

"Tanya was here, when he came; he had no quarrel with Tanya. But how could they have got hold of the poison, if it was still in the locket around Tanya's neck?

"Oh, this is a horrible case. No that's wrong! Lady Emily is a horrible woman! That's the truth of the matter." Peters sighed and wearily looked at his sergeant.

"Pierce, Manders must be back by now, with Bert's witness. I'll go and get this damn 'Bert Liveridge episode' over.

"See Stephen Armitage for me and just confirm *when* he arrived; I think it'll be about eleven o'clock, or soon after; ask whether he saw Liveridge in the bar; what exactly did he do; – you know the drill.

"Now, for that blasted bugger, Liveridge and ... the other bloke, what's his name? ...Oh yes, I've got it: Alf Cookson."

CHAPTER 19

Inspector Peters, coming from the hall to the small parlour, almost bumped into Mr Herbert Norman, the Presbyterian Minister. They both stopped, with mutual apologies.

Herbert was well known to the inspector – both well known and respected. They had been closely involved in a previous tragic case in the village. Peters admired Herbert: a very good and decent man.

"Mr Norman," he cried, "I didn't expect to see you, but happy to do so."

"Likewise, Inspector," replied Herbert smiling, "I'm here with one of my parishioners, sir, Mr Alfred Cookson. He was nervous about this meeting and asked if I would come with him. I tried to assure him, Inspector, he had nothing to fear from you, but you know how it is …"

"Indeed, I'm glad you're here. Let's go over here, for a moment, away from everyone. I want to have a word with you, about the legal problems of this situation and what I think is the best way to handle it. I would be grateful for your opinion."

"Certainly, it's yours, if you think it's of any worth." The two men moved to one side of the hall and spoke in whispers. They then collected Alf Cookson, then went in to Bert Liveridge and a weary-looking, Constable Potts. Peters immediately sent Potts home, but retained Manders, to take notes.

The clergyman and the inspector, sat behind the desk, facing

Bert Liveridge and Alf Cookson – an elderly, thin tall man with a cadaverous face and a bushy moustache. His eyes were clear and intelligent.

"Now," began Peters in his official voice, "I have had a very busy and exhausting day and I will not tolerate any nonsense, or any pre-varication. If you do not cooperate fully and truthfully, I shall arrest you both and take you to the police station. Is that clear?"

The men nodded; Alf Cookson looking terrified.

"This is how we shall proceed. You, Liveridge, shall repeat all you told us previously and you, Mr Cookson, shall listen intently. If there is any discrepancy, you must tell us instantly. I have brought Mr Norman in with me. You both know him well and respect him. He is here as my witness, both as to what is said and the legal process that I am following."

He looked hard at Bert Liveridge. "Right, off you go." Constable Manders had his book open; soon his pencil was flying as he recorded in his impeccable shorthand, every word that was uttered.

When Bert Liveridge had finished, Peters turned to Cookson. "Well?"

Alf Cookson cleared his throat. "I think, sir, that's about all of it. I think Bert has told the complete truth of what was said, as he remembers it. However, there were a couple of things that I noted."

"Yes?"

"Well, after Miss Ilich had made the infamous suggestion to my neighbour – which I might add nearly caused me to have a heart attack on the spot – and what a place to have that in!

"Anyhow ... after she had spoken, Bert kept saying, over and over and over: 'ten thousand pounds.' I personally believe that the amount of money was the most surprising thing to him at the time. It was only later, it seemed to me, that he realised what he had been asked to do."

"However, he was aware enough, to ask the *details* of how the murder was to be done, wasn't he?" reminded the Inspector.

"Oh, dear, so he was – I didn't think of that. However, I'd like to add a word to help my friend and neighbour. When Bert came back to the bar room, I told him I had heard him, but all he could keep saying, was the amount of money – ten thousand pounds."

"And you threatened him, Mr Cookson?"

"Well, I suppose you could call it that. I told him I was going to tell my Minister all about it, because I didn't know what I should do; I've never been in such a situation before in my life.

"I thought Bert should go straight to the police, but he objected and said he intended seeing the young woman the next morning and telling her it was not on – he had no intention of killing anyone. And…" Alf began to sweat in his agitation.

"I have to tell you, sir, that Bert is not *capable* of killing anyone. I don't care if it embarrasses him, or not, if I tell you, but all the years I have been his neighbour, he has asked me to kill his chickens; he can't even do that – it's the same with rabbits …"

"All right, all right, Alf, you don't have to go, on and on, about it …" grumbled Bert, red faced.

Peters was secretly amused at Bert's discomfit, but keeping his voice cold, he said: "You are very fortunate in your friends, Mr Liveridge; more than you deserve.

"You have been blinded by the fantastic amount of money, and I believe, without realising the seriousness of what you were doing, you entered into a conspiracy to murder – and you gave tacit consent – that means, you did not refuse *vocally* at the time, but kept *silent*.

"However, Mr Norman and I have discussed this situation and I am going to place you on your honour – in his presence – and demand that you give me your word, that you have spoken the whole and complete truth. I ask you to swear it by all you hold most sacred.

"You, Mr Cookson, will swear before God: you, Mr Liveridge, according to what you hold most sacred. What would that be, Mr Cookson?"

"For my friend, Inspector, that would undoubtedly be the memory of his good mother – on his mother's grave. Would that do?"

"Certainly," answered Peters. The two men dutifully did as requested. Peters stood up and dismissed both of them. When they had left the room, he spent a few moments talking with his old friend.

"It's pretty weird, Herbert," he remarked wryly, "a bit like a court of law – I just hope they don't realise I *don't* have the authority to do, what I just *did*.

"I suppose I could be reported for what I have done, but the truth is, I don't really believe that silly old Bert, actually meant to carry out any murderous activity."

"He's all talk and theories, Inspector," agreed the Minister, "I've known him a long time – a constant complainer and whinger, but on the whole, an honest and decent enough man."

"Oh well, that's one thing out of the way. It was good to see you again, Herbert. Is your wife Alice well?"

"Thanks be to God, wonderfully well and happy – which is such a great blessing after what happened in the past. Annie Watson did the trick by taking Alice to the nursery at the Orphanage. Alice is in her element there. I live in constant fear she's going to bring home about fourteen babies all at once!"

Herbert laughed happily. "The Orphanage work was the best thing that could ever have happened to her."

"You cannot realise how happy that makes me, Herbert. We see such tragedies in this job. Thank God, as you say, that good can come out of what seemed pure evil, at the time.

"Perhaps even this dreadful, never-ending war, may bring about some good? …No, don't take any notice of that remark, Herbert; I think that's stretching things too far – with all the terrible suffering and loss of life …"

The two men chatted on current war news; particularly the very real threat now of a Japanese invasion; how helpless Australia was, if that came to pass; how terrible it was to feel so impotent in the face of such a horrific threat.

When the two men had finished talking, Mr Norman drove Alf and Bert back home, in his buggy, while Peters and Constable Manders, returned to the police station in Tavistock.

***

"Betty," Mr Jones called as he saw the young woman hurry past the open door of his office. She stopped, with a tray of glasses in her arms. "No, go and put those on the bar, and if you're free, could you spare me a couple of minutes, girl?"

"Be with you Joe, in a jiffy," Betty replied. When she had dumped the tray, she hurried back to the office. She was very fond of both Joe and his wife, Biddy and was aware that the landlord looked very anxious. What could have gone wrong now? Perhaps it was yet another of those blasted Government forms. She came into the office.

"Please sit down Betty, I've something to tell you."

"Good gracious, Joe, you're not ill are you? You do look a funny colour. Do you want me to get Biddy?"

"No, dear, she knows what I'm going to say to you." Betty looked alarmed. Surely she was not going to be sacked. She loved the old pub, and enjoyed working there – it was her home. She clasped her hands together tightly.

"Betty this is rather difficult for me to say, but, well … I'm not much good at making speeches … The truth of the matter is …"

Ten minutes later, Betty came out of the office, her eyes like saucers, and her legs wobbly. She went into the bar, and was so grateful there was no one there. She sat down quickly on one of the stools, her mind struggling to come to grips with the fact that she was going to be, on Joe's retirement at the end of the war, a full partner in the business, and on his death, the outright owner – lock, stock and barrel – of the Sheridan Inn! Joe and Biddy had left everything to her!

CHAPTER 20

Telephone call from Annie Watson to Hannah Kelly at the dairy: "Hannah? … Are you free for a minute? Good! Did you get your Women's Land Army girls? … You did? That was fast! You threatened that horrible milk inspector? I'm delighted, he deserved it; cosy job he's got – he doesn't have to get up at four in the morning!

"What are the girls like? Sally? Nice old fashioned name … Oh dear, nothing old fashioned about *her*! … She isn't? *Fourteen* stone! Good God, how do you feed her? … But a good worker; well that's all that matters, isn't it? …She actually *can* milk? Came from a farm; you've been lucky there. What about the other one? … Oh dear … really? Paints her nails … frightened of getting them broken? … Yes, I can see she'd be a great help to you, on the farm! …You've given her, WHAT? …She's responsible for the mucking out? … No, dear, that's me laughing, Hannah; I'm sure you'll sort her out – that'll fix her nails! How's Dan coping with them? … Can't stand them? Well, I suppose, it's safer, that way …

"Oh, that's a surprise! So the signs are pointing in a new direction? Well, Bianca's a lovely girl, and it's a very good family; I think it's outrageous that the men are interned. So, Joan's not in the picture any more? Well, I know you must be disappointed, but … pardon? You're not? Oh? You'd prefer Bianca? Yes, I understand: same sort of background; understands work … yes, that's true, I *do* see that.

"Now, dear, that's enough gossiping. I've something serious

to discuss with you; it's about Amelia Tatley. I think that dreadful woman, my relative, has caused great distress to that dear, kind and wonderful old lady ... Well, dear so do I – Amelia's been a wonderful neighbour to us, all these years.

"Do you happen to know where she came from? ...No, I don't either, but I think I'll have to find out; there's something wrong. I spoke to Amelia after she had finished being questioned at the pub; she was in tears ... No, not from the police, but about something else altogether ... It is terrible – another person in fearful distress, because of *that* woman ...

"Hannah, you know I rely on your common sense so much – not having any of my own ... Well, that's as may be. To be serious, dear, do you think I should have a word with Inspector Peters, for I've had an idea? ... Yes, another one I'm afraid ... It's about the poison ... Yes, hydrogen cyanide; it was carried around the Russian's neck, in that gold locket, she wore ... You didn't know? I thought everyone knew by now. Well, it was that particular cyanide that killed her and I think I know how it was done. No, that's not true! I can *guess* how it was done ... You think I should? All right; if he chews me out, I'll say it was your idea.

"Thanks dear, love to Dan and make sure he keeps his distance from those girls – especially the lazy one who paints her nails – they're the dangerous ones! ... Bye, dear."

***

Major Tim Johnson entered the pub and, instead of going into the bar, went in search of Mr Jones. He ran him to earth in the cellars.

Joe was surprised; he knew and liked Major Johnson, but the major had never been down in the cellars before. When Tim found the landlord, the elderly man was struggling with a large cask. Tim immediately came to Joe's assistance and the two men soon finished the work that had to be done down there. Joe told Tim that it deserved a beer on the house and they were about to go up the cellar stairs, when Tim stopped. He was clearly embarrassed.

"Mr Jones, I must speak to you. Please wait a moment." Joe turned round surprised. "You see, I know that Betty has no father – I know her good mother well, of course – the cook, down at the hospital – so, before I speak to Betty I wanted to talk to you. I understand Betty has been with you for years?"

"Indeed, she has, Major, ever since she left school. Like a daughter to the wife and me."

"That's what I thought. Well, the fact is, I'm in love with Betty – have been for months, but haven't been able to get up the courage to speak to her." The landlord's eyes began to twinkle; he beamed at the young man.

"I thought the wind was blowing strongly in that direction, sir," he smiled. "But what's stopping you speaking to her?"

"It's this wretched illness, Mr Jones. That's the problem. I don't know whether it's fair to ask any woman to have to cope with that. What happens if I have a relapse; if I had to go back to a hospital? If the nightmares begin again? Or, God forbid, that I have to have more Electric Shock Treatment?"

Joe Jones was moved with pity for the young soldier. How unfair everything is, he reflected. This is a fine man, learned too, Betty said, and did well in the army – promoted to a major – and now after fighting more than three years, left with nerves shot to hell.

"Son," the old man said, "I don't know much about those kinds of illnesses, but why should they be any different from any other illness. You could have been badly shot, and in a couple of years, find yourself crippled with arthritis – who can tell what's going to happen to any of us?

"What seems to me to be more important at the moment is – now that you are finished with all the treatment – is that you'll be *transferred*, won't you?" Tim nodded.

"Well, I think *where* you're going to be sent, is more important than the illness, you have had. I really don't know whether this is right or not, but it seems unfair to me, to put a ring on a girl's finger and ask her to wait and wait for years, for someone who may, never ever, come home again."

"Well, that's no problem, Mr Jones, as I do know what they're going to do with me. I received the news this morning. I'm going to be honourably discharged on medical grounds. Dr Gascoigne-Ridley recommended this, after he examined me the last time. So, the war's over, as far as I am concerned."

"Well, I heartily thank God for that, Major. I was dreading that you'd be sent back to the front lines – it's vicious hand-to-hand fighting in the Pacific now, so I hear. It's been worrying us sick, the missus and me. And," he added smiling, "Betty, very much so."

"Really, Mr Jones? Betty was worried?"

"Of course she was, son. She cares for you, anyone can see that."

"And you'd have no objection to me speaking to her; to ask her to marry me?"

"Of course, I haven't. She is a fine and wonderful girl, with brains as well and you're a good and decent chap. What more could we want? I know the only thing that will upset the missus and me as well, is the thought of Betty going away from here. However, she has her own life to lead and her place will be with her husband – we understand that."

"Well, what I was thinking was, if Betty will have me, I would like to stay in this area. I've come to like the village and the people here – they've been very good to me; I'd like to stay, if I could find somewhere to live."

"Really? Well, that's even better news. Well son, off you go! Betty should be in the bar by now, getting ready to open. Go and speak to her now. Don't put it off any longer and try not to worry about the illness.

"As our dear and beloved Lady Mary Sheridan, used to say about every problem: just leave it in the hands of God."

CHAPTER 21

Telephone call from Annie Watson to Inspector Peters:
"Oh, you're there, Inspector, I was hoping you would be, even though it's Saturday. Well, of course it's Annie, the eternal busy-body … You're very kind to say so. No it's nothing sensational, but I'd like to ask a couple of questions if I may; I know I've no right at all to do so, but being the insatiably curious person that I am … Well, that's very nice of you; not true, of course, but then compliments rarely are true, are they?

"The thing is, I think I can guess how the cyanide, got from Tanya's locket, into her drink … Yes, I think I *do* know, but, before I tell you my deduction – no that's ridiculous – my wild *guess* – that's more like it – I want to ask you something; is that a deal? … You're not allowed to make deals with us, poor lay-folk? …What a load of baloney! I'm making deals all the time; otherwise, we'd starve to death … No, it's not all *that* different … Anyhow, I'll ask you my questions and you can refuse to answer if you like; how about that?

"Well, what I want to know is this: did other people know that Lady Emily took a short walk in the blackout, each night? …The answer is, yes? That's wasn't too painful was it? My second question is even easier: did you know, that just about everyone now knows, about Tanya hitting the jackpot and getting all the lovely money? … *How* did *I* know that?

"My dear man, you've obviously never lived in a village, if you thought that'd remain a secret. We've all been talking of it ever since Bert was arrested … Well, not *arrested* then, 'assisting the police in their enquiries,' is that better? …

"Yes, of course Bert and Alf talked; the most exciting thing that's happened to them in their lives; they told Lily, as a dead secret, who told Hannah, as a dead secret, who told Bianca, as a dead secret – need I go on? …I didn't think so …Now one last question: All the people who went to the pub to see Emily, said she had 'phoned them; apparently, she had something she wanted to tell them. Did you find out what those things were, as many told me, she had nothing to tell them?

"Something's wrong somewhere, isn't it? … No comment? … All right, you've answered my questions, so pin back your ears, Inspector, for here's my wild theory – it might be crazy, but I truly think it's the right answer … …"

Annie hung up the receiver with mixed feelings. Well, at least, the inspector hadn't laughed at her; but then he wouldn't, she reasoned; he's a very polite chap with perfect manners. Oh, it's just possible I'm right, but it's equally possible, I'm dead wrong. She picked up the Latin textbook and went back to Billy's room.

Billy was much better, and was siting in an easy chair, near the window of his room. He was reading and looked up expectantly, as his mother entered the room.

"Have you found it?" he asked eagerly.

"Yes. To tell the truth, Billy, I was going to pretend that I couldn't find it. Son, I can't pretend that I'm of much help – at this standard of Latin."

"Not to worry, Mum. We'll manage; it's not that difficult."

"So you say. Well, I can but try … Oh! Who's that calling me? Excuse me Billy." Annie hurried out to the kitchen to the back door; she had heard the voice coming from there.

To her surprise, it was Amelia Tatley, her usual strong and confident voice tremulous, her face ashen. Annie immediately welcomed her old friend and with her arm around her, brought her in and settled her at the kitchen table. The kettle was switched on, and Annie was busy quickly assembling things necessary for morning tea.

There was silence in the room, until both women were sitting at the table. Annie noticed, for the first time, that Amelia was holding an envelope. Even at a distance it was clear that it was made of very expensive paper and had a crest of some sort on it.

Annie experienced a sinking feeling, as she recognized the crest. If there's a letter with a crest, she knew, it would be from that wretched Lady Emily.

"What is it, Amelia?" Annie asked. "I recognize the crest on your envelope. I fear that you have further bad news from that fiendish relative of mine. Is that so?"

Instead of answering directly, Amelia looked closely at her friend. "Annie, how long have I been here now – in Bexforth North?"

"Heavens, I don't know, Amelia. Long before I married, for I remember you coming to the Big House, to visit Mother and me. We've been friends for more than twenty years, I think."

"It's twenty-seven years, this year," Amelia confirmed. "And you have always treated me, as if I were one of the family; I've never told you how much I appreciate that."

Annie waved it away. "Rubbish! You've been a damn good friend to me and to half the village as well, Amelia," she reached across the table, and took the elderly, arthritic, hands. "Look, dear, what is all this about? You can tell me; you can tell me anything. What has that ghastly woman been writing to you?"

"You don't really know anything at all about me, do you Annie," Amelia stated. "You don't know where I came from, what I was before I came here, or what I was doing?"

"Why should I? You've always been the same decent, good woman – a neighbour whom I cherish. Now, if you're going to tell me that you were once a bank robber, or the sister of Jack the Ripper,

I won't be horrified, I'd most probably say, 'how exciting'.

"But, tell me, what has that odious woman said to upset you?"

"Annie, she knows who I *was*. She has said that if I do not come to the inn to see her tomorrow morning, and agree to her conditions, she will not only reveal the truth about me, but see that the newspapers publish my real name."

"But, I don't understand. Your name is Amelia …"

"No, it isn't, Annie. It's Lucy …"

"Stop!" shouted Annie, "I don't want to know."

"Annie, you *have* to know. It's *Lucy* …"

Annie blocked her ears. "No, you are *Amelia Tatley* to me, and that's what you'll always be. Whatever you've done in the past, is no business of mine – *if* you've done anything which I doubt – you have had an honourable life and a wonderful record of forty years teaching. That is a great and glorious achievement. What happened before that – why, you must have been a mere girl – is of no consequence."

Annie was very angry. She reached for the envelope. "Please Amelia let me read what that woman has written – I think she's evil. It's an *exorcist* she needs, more than anyone else."

Amelia silently handed the letter to Annie, who scanned the lines quickly, her own face growing white, while her teeth clenched with fury at what her relative had done. She laid the letter down slowly.

"Amelia – yes, I'll continue calling you that to the end of your life. It's your legal name – the other's utterly unimportant." Annie pondered silently, for a minute what to do, and then came to a decision.

"Tomorrow morning, Amelia, you will not be going *alone* to Lady Emily. I shall be with you. While she is apparently ready to publicly accuse you, I shall have a few words to say to her first.

"Yes, we'll see her together. She'll know you're not without friends and that you have the total support of me. You realise all this is just to attack me, don't you? She attacks and ruins my friends, knowing that I'll grieve over it; so now she's turned her attention to you, knowing that we're close.

"Just a minute," she picked up the letter again, "I see, you're to be there at half past nine, right. Where? Oh, I see, she demands that you go up to her sitting room – that's between the two bedrooms. Amelia," again Annie took Amelia's hands in her own, "you realise that Inspector Peters must know of this?" Amelia nodded.

"It's proof positive of blackmail, which is a criminal offence. Would you like me to contact Inspector Peters for you? Let's consider that done, shall we." Annie sat up straight again.

"Now, if you've finished, Amelia, please come and speak to Billy; he'll be so disappointed if you don't." Amelia put her head down on the table, and wept quietly. Annie sensibly left her alone for a few minutes, then led her gently into the boy's bedroom.

Billy, with his usual enthusiasm, greeted his old friend joyfully and for the next twenty minutes regaled Amelia with stories about what he had been reading, which brought back a smile, to her ravaged face.

When she was about to leave, Amelia leant over and kissed Billy, to his great surprise. Before he could recover, she had quickly gone from the room and left the house.

***

Annie stood near the phone working out what she was to say to the police. This could be exceedingly tricky. Do I have any right to go ahead with this, she wondered? What if I'm completely *wrong*? Perhaps it's just that I like interfering so much … but, if I'm *right* and don't interfere, who else is there to help Amelia? There's *no one* else.

And, dear God, the *gossip*! If anyone in this village found out she

was living under an assumed name! But they *mustn't*! Please God …
they *must* NOT!

In her agitation, she jerked the curtain near the phone. This
room looked out directly across to Amelia Tatley's house.

Her eyes opened wide in disbelief and outrage – the Estate
Agents were hammering a 'For Sale' notice into the ground of
Amelia Tatley's front garden!

Suddenly stung into action and in a barely-controlled fury,
Annie dialled the police. It was answered immediately.

"Get me Inspector Peter, this is Annie Watson. It is vitally urgent
and I will not be put off with anyone else...

"And … just *hurry* … damn you … damn you, damn you. Stop
dithering. *Hurry!*"

CHAPTER 22

It was exactly half-past nine o'clock, as Annie stood by the side of Amelia Tatley outside the door of Lady Emily's sitting room. The women looked briefly at each other, nodded, then Annie rapped smartly on the door.

A light, tuneful voice called for them, to 'enter'. They found Lady Emily sitting gracefully at the table, beautifully dressed in her new mourning clothes, with her large, black, leather handbag, on the table in front of her. She let loose a peal of delighted laughter, when she saw Annie.

"I *knew* she would bring *you*," crowed the woman. "In this god-forsaken village there is no show without Punch, is there? There has to be a *Sheridan* present – damn the whole tribe of them! No, you needn't sit; you won't be here long."

"Perhaps a little longer than you expect, Emily," replied Annie quietly.

"Nonsense, I have a little arrangement to make with Miss '*Tatley*'; it has nothing at all to do with you."

"I'm afraid it has everything to do with me. But, let's leave that for a moment, Emily. Would you please tell me why are you doing all this? What is it all for? Is it about me?"

Emily's face twisted into a grimace of hate. "Oh *course*, it's about *you*!"

"Why for Heaven's sake? What have I ever done to you? I don't understand. If it's all about me, why are you attacking everyone else?"

"Because I loathe and detest you, and the whole smug Sheridan clan, that's why. I've hated you ever since I was unfortunate enough to enter your family, by marrying John.

"As soon as I did that, I never stopped hearing of, 'the lovely Anne'; 'the clever Anne'; 'the aristocratic Anne'. Everyone was talking about *you* – the loved darling of the Sheridan family – not about *me*, the *nothing*. You, the clever doyen of a great house; *me* – who had nothing but beauty and fabulous wealth – *that* didn't count!

"*Didn't count!* Even though the decayed glories of the Sheridans were, in fact, a sham: they were *bankrupt*! Oh, yes, my lady, it's about you, all right. I swore I'd get my own back on you, by destroying all those you cared for … and I *will.*"

"Have you ever thought, Emily, what John, your late husband, would think of all this?"

"*Him*! The only decent thing he ever did in his life was to get a knighthood. Once that had happened, he didn't last long. Her voice changed. She leant forward slightly.

"Heart condition, you know," she added, confidentially, woman to woman, "had to take special tablets. It was dead easy to increase the tablets, so that he had an unexpected turn, and I was left the inconsolable widow.

"Do you know what happened? It was exactly as Oscar Wilde had said, in one of his naughty plays: 'my hair turned quite gold, from grief!" She leant back, laughing aloud uncontrollably in her exultation.

"You *killed* John?"

"Of course! He was of no further use to me …"

"He had given you a beautiful daughter …"

"*Her*! An ingrate! Thinks of nothing but her revolting children! However, I'll deal with her; I have a plan for dealing with those snivelling brats. When they're gone, she'll be sorry she threw me out of her house."

"Emily," Annie said softly, suddenly aware that she was in the room, with a dangerous woman: perhaps, even a psychopathic killer. She realised they were in danger. If …perhaps … if she kept the woman talking? …that might be the best thing to do. She looked at the manic woman with compassion.

"Emily, Monica is a lovely daughter – you know that. Why did she ask you to leave her house? She's very fond of you, I know."

"She had this trumped up excuse that I was ruining her marriage. Did you ever hear anything so ridiculous?" Emily asked incredulously.

"Just because I took up three rooms, in their squalid little house; Monica and the Beast had to sleep on the back verandah …"

"The Beast?"

"That clown of an engineer, she married. I was determined that that would not last. All he did was father three runny-nosed brats – he has to go; I'm determined on that."

Annie was startled by the extent of Emily's insanity – the woman was clearly stark raving mad. But, being Annie, as usual she couldn't help a surge of sympathy for this demented woman.

"Emily," she interrupted, "why didn't you go and see Lady Benedicta? She is a good and wise woman, as well as being a nun …"

"Her! I *did* go, you fool. Do you know what she told *me* to do? She said that the only way I could win salvation, was to get a job in a munition factory and learn to *work*!

"*ME*! Work in a *factory*! … I think she's insane!

"I instructed her, instantly, to take my name off her list of patrons and she had the nerve to tell me it would be a relief to do so, because my name took up too much space on the letterhead!

"But, that's beside the point; I have to make these arrangements with Amelia Tatley."

"Just a moment, Emily. I want to know about Tanya Illich."

"What about her?"

"Well," Annie began apologetically, "just a little thing really: *why did YOU murder her?*"

Emily half rose in her chair, staring at Annie, her eyes wide with amazement. "You *knew*?"

"Of course, I knew. It was quite infantile, really …"

"*Infantile!*" Emily actually screeched in her outrage. "*Infantile!*"

"Yes, infantile! How stupid to use that cyanide from the locket. I suppose you stole it one night when Tanya was sleeping, didn't you? She would take the locket off at night and it would be easy to slip into her room, unscrew the little locket, remove the capsule and keep it handy.

"Tanya would never know; it was not one of those things that you would keep opening to look at, out of sentiment."

"But, how did you guess it was I who took the poison?"

"Really, Emily, give me some credit for common sense. It could only have been one of two people – you or Tanya. Either Tanya committed suicide, or else you took the capsule and used it later.

"That was clear to me from the beginning. What held me up was trying to understand why *you* wanted to kill your – supposedly – best friend."

"You'll never guess why I did that."

"I'm afraid I already have, Emily. You see I know about the Will. A Will is worthless unless it is *signed*; when I heard that you had a Will *drawn up, but not yet signed*, I knew it had to be you. You were testing Tanya weren't you?"

"Yes, I was. That traitorous brat, taken from the gutter and she would sell me for ten thousand pounds, would she! I have no remorse, whatsoever. I hate her even more than I hate you.

"You see, I began to doubt her a month ago when I saw her looking at me, when she was unaware I could see her. There was cold speculation in her eyes."

"And so you thought up the idea of the Will?"

"Yes, I thought I would find out, one way, or the other. I didn't have to wait long. The very next night after I had told her about the

Will, I overheard her talking to that weasel – 'Bert …Something' – outside, when I was taking my evening walk in the dark – to spite that fat moron, the publican.

"She actually asked that bucolic, 'Bert', yokel, to hit me on the head, for ten thousand pounds! Ten thousand pounds – *she was going to sell me for a piffling ten thousand pounds!*"

"Emily, it was fortunate for you, that you had enraged so many village people, that they were prepared to come, when you summonsed them here, on the fatal morning. You phoned them – to prepare an alibi, to conceal your part, in the murder, didn't you?

"You were the one who demanded the police regard the death as murder, so you had to have a murderer. So, the innocent people *did* turn up, as you planned – to be your scapegoats – and you changed places with Tanya, at the last moment. That was a bit risky wasn't it?"

"Not really. I'd arranged that this creature here – this, so-called 'Tatley' woman – would be the last person to see me 'alive' and when Tanya had come in earlier, I told her to come down at eleven o'clock precisely, through the back corridor and I would leave her favourite drink waiting for her on the table.

"She came, tripping in like a lamb to the slaughter. I had cut the top off the capsule with my nail scissors and poured the cyanide into the gin. I left the drink on the table, and went out the back corridor and up the back stairs."

Emily laughed again, happily, then her voice changed. She looked earnestly at the two women, and added, confidentially:

"Well, I had to, you see. I knew all the people would be turning up soon to see the corpse and I had to change into a completely different outfit and repair my makeup."

"Yes, I do understand, Emily," murmured Annie shakily, "you wanted to look your best! But tell me about Tanya? Where did the poor girl come from? Did she have parents?"

"Well, she *did* have," Emily laughed, again, this time uproariously. "When we first met I was very interested in her fervour, so she took me back to meet her parents. They had a house – a tiny terrace, in an inner city slum – horrible place. And do you know what happened?

"As soon as they heard I was involved in the movement – they called it the '*Red* Movement' – they refused to let me in! Me! They refused to let *ME* into their *hovel*!

"I was not going to stand for that. They had a little tobacconist kiosk nearby – you know one of those peculiar things like a caravan, with a flap in the front which becomes the counter, with only one door to the thing. They sold newspapers and cigarettes." Lady Emily paused, smiling as she remembered.

"Yes?"

"Well, a friend of mine had taught me how to make Molotov cocktails – he was sweet – so I practised and then, a few days later, I threw one at the door of their kiosk; it burst into flames immediately and they were burnt to death."

Emily laughed helplessly. "Oh dear, I can't help laughing, but you should have seen the mother – a huge fat woman – trying to climb over the counter, with her hair and clothes alight."

Annie made a retching sound in her throat, holding on to the back of a chair to steady herself. Amelia stared at the woman in front of her, as if she were in the presence of the devil himself. Both women were white with shock. The laughing suddenly ceased. Emily looked seriously at Amelia and spoke coldly.

'I've become distracted. I have to deal with Amelia. I know all about you, Miss, and what you have done.

"Here are my conditions for my silence: you will withdraw your house from sale – I saw the ridiculous sign – tomorrow, when the Estate Agents reopen and your house will become the headquarters, in this district, for the Advancement of Communism.

"There will be a large sign to that effect in your front garden; your name will be listed there as the Secretary."

Amelia was so stunned by the demands, that in spite of the

horror of the situation, she began to smile grimly. "Really, Lady Emily, you must be insane if you think I would do that. I have made my own plans. I am leaving this area tomorrow; I spent last night packing, what I would take with me.

"With the sale of my little cottage, together with my savings, that will be enough for me to be able to live in lodgings until I die. I will not shame my neighbours in this way, no matter what threats you use against me."

Lady Emily sighed. "Well, you now leave me no alternative, you silly woman, do you? Though I don't really blame *you*; it's not really your fault; it's that wretched Annie Watson who's to blame – you're under her influence. Yes," Emily's brow furrowed in thought. She picked up her large handbag.

Suddenly, she came to a decision. "Yes, it would be better if *she* has to go as well; she's the cause of all the problems in my life. Yes, it's the only way – the criminal first and then the famous *Annie Watson!*" Emily laughed gleefully. "*She'll* never be famous again!" She took her hand out of the large handbag. It was now holding a pearl-handled revolver.

Both women took a hurried step backwards.

"Emily," Annie shouted, loudly. "*Put the gun away*! For the love of God, think what you are doing! How do you think you can get away with this?"

"Quite easily! I shall shoot Amelia, then you; place the revolver in her hand, and scream loudly. I'll tell the police Amelia shot you and then killed herself. The police are so stupid they'll believe anything – especially from someone as respectable and as *wealthy*, as I."

Still chatting in a natural manner, Lady Emily checked her weapon expertly, raised the revolver and steadied her aim.

Annie screamed and threw herself at the demented woman struggling to get control of the gun; Emily grappled madly and furiously with Annie, but – with the gun waving about in an extremely dangerous manner – with her manic strength, Emily still managed to keep the gun pointed at Amelia. The room exploded into sound as she fired two shots which ploughed into the body of the poor, defenceless elderly woman.

Amelia crashed to the floor, while Annie, with a violent heave, pulled down the arm of the insane and screaming woman reefing the weapon from the hand. As the door burst open, however, when Emily, shrieking madly, saw the police pouring into the room, she made one last desperate grab for the gun.

For one terrible moment, both Annie's and Emily's hands were on the gun fighting for control of the weapon which Emily was directing mainly in the direction of the door. Annie thought she had it, but at the last moment it slipped almost entirely from her hand and Emily had just grabbed it when it suddenly fired filling the room with ear-deafening sound.

Annie, heard a stifled scream from Constable Manders. Spinning round, she was horrified as she glimpsed the young man clutching his arm – from which blood was sprouting. Her mind was reeling: who had fired the gun? Had *she* shot a policeman?

Annie, swinging back to Emily, with a final wrench, panting dreadfully, she managed to drag the gun from the mad woman's hand and hurled it into the corner of the room.

The bullet had gone through the skin of Manders's left arm, then through the open door, smashing two large windows which gave light to the upper floor. There was a shattering crash of glass hitting the pavement below, while the report of the shots startled everyone in the village.

Terrified, people – not knowing what was happening, began to run in the direction of the pub.

Peters scooped up the gun from the floor, shoved it into his pocket and helped Pierce and Watkins as they struggled with the frenzied Lady Emily.

Annie's eyes began to lose focus; she looked at Inspector Peters vaguely and muttered: "What kept you?" as she shakily knelt by the side of her life-time friend.

Pierce and Constable Watkins, finally managed to overcome Emily. In the struggle, Emily had tried to bite and kick the police. Her hair was now a disaster, her makeup in tatters: the lipstick smeared across her cheeks, the mascara in blotchy smudges around her eyes.

They handcuffed her and forced her into a chair, Pierce holding her firmly until Watkins was able to get one leg handcuffed to the chair.

Emily stared balefully at the police and now with the outer mask removed she looked what she was – an evil, insane, and vicious killer.

***

Constable Potts took no part in the apprehension of Emily, but sat down on the floor instantly, cradling the dying Amelia – his old friend of twenty years – in his arms.

The blood was starting to trickle from the corners of Amelia's mouth. It dripped onto Potts' hand, unheeded, where it was diluted by the tears from the elderly Constable.

Constable Potts was weeping.

Amelia's eyes opened. Her eye-lashes fluttered as she looked up. Her eyes were pleading. She attempted to speak. Potts bent down as far as he could. Amelia's lips opened; "Father, do … you … forgive … me, now?" she whispered panting.

Potts was startled to be confused by the dying woman with her own long-dead father, but answered instantly:

"Yes, my child, I forgive you totally." Amelia smiled happily, her eyes became fixed and a deep gurgle of blood began in her throat and spilled out of her mouth. The constable never relaxed his hold for a second, as Amelia died.

The silence was broken by Peters. He spoke to Annie who was kneeling by the side of the dead Amelia, praying for her beloved neighbour. Peters touched Annie's shoulder gently.

"I've read the letter Mrs Watson, so this is *Lucy* …"

Annie's head cleared suddenly. Her clear strong voice rang out loudly, overruling the inspector: "No, Inspector, this is *Amelia Hephzibah Tatley*, spinster of this parish … beloved friend and neighbour … She *is Amelia Tatley*; God rest her beautiful, precious soul." Annie quietly began to weep, rocking to, and fro, in her anguish.

"That's right," Peters corrected himself hastily, his face white. "I'm sorry, Mrs Watson. That's right. *This is Miss Amelia Tatley*."

At Peters' voice, Annie looked up; her eyes suddenly focused on the Inspector:

"What kept you?" she repeated weakly, just as her daughter Penny and young George McKenzie ran into the room, both shouting her name frantically.

***

"What kept you? That's what you asked me, Mrs Watson," Inspector Peters paused to accept a cup of tea from Penelope Watson.

He and Sergeant Pierce were seated with the Watson family at their kitchen table. Annie was seated in an easy chair near the table and her husband, Sam, was holding her hand tightly, while Billy was back in bed.

He was very distressed by the death of his friend, Amelia and had asked to be left alone, but young George went in, and was talking to him quietly. It was three hours after the scene at the pub.

"Well, I *would* like to know, Inspector. I couldn't understand why it took you so long to get into the room. I knew you were in the next room – in Tanya's room – but I expected you earlier – I was running out of ideas of what to say."

Peters sighed. "It was one of those things that can always happen in a difficult situation – ridiculous, even funny, in hindsight, but a *nightmare* while it's happening: the wretched old door jammed on us – the door of Tanya's room. We nearly went crazy trying to get the wretched thing to open, and couldn't budge it, until it was too late."

Annie nodded. "Well, perhaps it was the *right timing* after all," she sighed. "Inspector, could you hear it all? I tried desperately to cover all the things I could think of that you would need, just to keep her talking."

"We heard perfectly and Constable Manders took it all down in his wonderful shorthand; it has all been typed up and the sergeant here, has copies for you to sign later."

'Poor Constable Manders! Was he badly hurt? Did I really shoot him, didn't I? Dear God, how could I do that? We were struggling for the wretched gun; I really can't remember the rest very well. I remember seeing his coat sleeve turning black from the blood …" Annie shivered and Sam held her closer. "Was he badly hurt?" she asked again, trembling.

"No, not badly at all thank Heaven. And, in all that thrashing about with you and Lady Emily locked in a deadly struggle I'm not really sure if you actually shot him, or whether Emily did, before you managed to get that damn gun away from her. I've decided that any ambiguity in the shooting will not be mentioned in my report.

"Anyway, the shot sliced through the muscle on his left arm but only superficially. It bled freely, and he suffered some shock, but Dr Kemp treated him on the spot and put in a couple of stitches – he'll be all right.

"Manders has a great sense of humour and while he was being brave – and trying not to flinch – as the doctor was probing the wound – he told me that he would now appear a hero to his girl friend, so he was quite happy to be shot in such a *safe* spot!" He laughed gently.

"And poor Constable Potts," Annie became tearful. "He was simply wonderful. He is a glorious human being, Inspector. It was clear that Amelia was something special in his eyes."

"He's unique all right," agreed Peters, while Pierce blew his nose loudly. "He told me he's known the lady from the first day she moved into her little cottage here, twenty-seven years ago. He thought she was, after Lady Mary, your mother, one of the finest women he had ever known."

"Does he need to know, Inspector?" Annie pleaded.

"Definitely not! Thank God you stopped me in time in that terrible room, Mrs Watson. I could have kicked myself; I had started to say Miss Tatley's real name – with Constables Manders, Watkins and Potts present. I would never have forgiven myself had I blurted out the surname."

"Please, I beg and entreat of you, *not* to tell me what Amelia had done – it must have been when she was a girl even younger than Penny and she has had an unblemished record for forty years as a teacher.

"I don't want to know her crime – if it was one and I assume it must have been – but I would like to know why she confused Constable Potts with her father."

"Well, I think I can tell you that," Peters answered. "Amelia did something tragically silly when she was about seventeen – for which she was charged and found guilty, but received a suspended sentence on account of her age.

"Her father, whom she adored, said she'd disgraced the family, so he changed the family's name by deed poll, moved to another state; sent Amelia to his sister to live and, thank God, his sister was a decent good woman – totally different from her brother.

"This aunt realised how clever Amelia was; made her sit for a scholarship examination for Teachers' College and set Amelia's feet on the path that she continued for forty years.

"Amelia's father never forgave his daughter – she never saw her family again. She's been alone all her life; totally from the time her aunt died. That was when she moved here to live."

"I see. Then, may God bless Constable Potts, for what he said to Amelia. She died thinking she was in the arms of her father and that he had forgiven her. Oh," Annie cried, "thank God for that! She was such a gentle, lovely woman."

Inspector Peters started to make moves to leave. "Mrs Watson, is there anything else you'd like to know before I go?"

"Did you have any idea it was Emily who killed Tanya, Inspector?"

"Only when she put on the great act of mourning, after I had asked her nephew to go and tell her that Tanya's death would be declared a suicide. She was frantic to persuade me that that was not so.

"I was puzzled. Why was she so insistent that it was murder? We thought it was murder, then had to come to grips with the fact that it wasn't. I admit we felt a little disappointed, which is silly I know. But I did think anyone would have been so relieved that it wasn't murder – sad as a suicide would be.

"I was also confused about the matter you mentioned on the phone. How come, if Emily had demanded attendance on her as she had special things to tell each individual she notified, not one of the people we interviewed even mentioned receiving any news?

"In fact, Emily refused to even talk to a few of them. It could have been, of course, that the details were so personal, or so shameful that *some* of them would be reluctant to speak of them, *but not all of them!* No, it didn't make sense.

"And then I wondered about the poison. I reasoned, as you did, that it must be one of the two women – it stood to reason that no one else would be able, easily, to get hold of that particular capsule, but I could find no link.

"I considered the possibility that Tanya had tried to murder her benefactress and something had gone wrong, then she'd drunk the poison herself, by mistake. I discarded that as being too fanciful.

"I thought, as you did, about the *unsigned* Will – it meant nothing, but I could not overlook it, it *might* have been genuine."

"No," Peters smiled, looking suddenly much younger, "we might have got there in the end, but, once again we are indebted to you … Pierce?"

"I'll say we are," seconded Pierce. "I couldn't believe what I was hearing while we were in the other room. The number of people that woman had killed! It fair took my breath away! And then, when the bloody – I beg your pardon – that damn door wouldn't open, after we heard you scream, I nearly went berserk, trying to get out."

Peters looked at Sam Watson.

"You have a remarkable wife there, Mr Watson," he declared.

Sam smiled, "I think she's too much for me, Inspector. She promised me after the last time, that all she wanted was to live a quiet life; actually *promised* me.

"I think I'll have to trade her in. When I heard the shots from the pub, I was over with Reg Cerney at the forge: That'll be the missus, I said, she's either been shot, or has just shot someone, so we didn't worry, just went on drinking beer."

"You're a big fibber, Sam Watson," Annie stated. "When I came to, in the pub, there you were, puffing like a grampus, with all your running."

Annie stood up, shakily. "Inspector, could I please read the statement and I'll sign it now. You have to get back I know."

Annie carefully read her statement and signed it with the two policemen signing as witnesses.

"Well, that's everything then," Inspector Peters said, gathering up the papers. "It was very nice to see you again Mr Watson." The policemen were taken to the front door by Penelope. As Peters shook hands with the young woman, he noticed that the engagement ring was back on her finger.

He smiled gently and left for the police station with Sergeant Pierce.

CHAPTER 23

It was one month later after the terrifying day on which Amelia was killed. Winter had set in with a vengeance in Bexford North, and heavy frosts were a regular feature of most mornings.

Annie was pleased, as she was now able to place all her pumpkins on the tin roofs of the sheds in the yard, so that they could be toughened by the frost; they would then last through the winter.

The villagers who had gardens had their root crops in – the carrots, parsnips, the turnips, the beetroot – and were carefully pickling the left-overs from the summer crops.

The cold weather seemed to bring about a renaissance of romance in the air. Penny and young George had met at the pub steps on that memorable Sunday, with Penny in terror for her mother's life. Together they had charged up the stairs and witnessed the end of the carnage, in that dreadful room. They had been inseparable ever since.

Dan Kelly had finally decided he had to face Joan Hennessy. He went to see her wondering how he could tell her about Bianca Firelli, only to discover that Joan had been trying to summons up courage to tell him she had fallen in love with a soldier in the hospital at The Junction. They were going to be married.

Mrs Hennessy had visited the soldier in the hospital and was very pleased with him, so had begun to think that perhaps it was better, after all, that Dan and Joan had broken off their understanding.

So, it was a very relieved Dan who drove home, went to see Bianca and her mother, and then asked permission to write to the father in the internees' camp, for permission to marry his daughter.

Hannah Kelly was delighted with the result. She was busy making plans for the wedding with her friend and neighbour, Mrs Firelli. Both women were also watching, with interest, the romance developing between Maria Firelli and the young Constable Watkins.

Dan thought it would be great to have a policeman, as a brother-in-law, but wondered, secretly, just what Mr Firelli would say about it, when he was released from internment, when the ghastly war finally was over.

***

Billy was settled once again in the empty fish shop with his new tutor, Major Tim Johnson and while there were a few difficult obstacles in the relationship to surmount in the beginning, they were now getting on fine.

Tim Johnson was happy to give Billy five mornings a week tutoring – and was aware that there was a sense of urgency now, as Billy's name had to be submitted in another month, in order to be able to sit, as a private student, for the matriculation examination itself and for one of the scholarships that were available.

Billy visited the Brady house whenever he could spare the time. Nan, Norah, Reg and Susan were always interested to hear how his studies were going. Once, when asked to mind baby Angela, for a few minutes, Billy began to read Latin and some Greek, to the infant. She seemed to like it, so he continued.

Reg, working at the forge, found that very funny. He, in his spare time, was building new rooms onto the back of Nan's stone cottage and Reg confided to Billy he and Susan were hoping for a large family.

This delighted Norah, who asked to be called 'Aunty' and loved, and was loved, by all. For the first time since Norah was born, Nan was free of anxiety, as to the future, of her beloved daughter. With Reg and Susan, Norah would have a home for as long as she lived.

In the afternoons, Tim worked at the pub, where he was now living, learning the hotel business from Mr Jones. When Tim had gathered up his courage and asked Betty to marry him, he had made clear to her, that he was fairly well off with an allowance from his family, so there would be no need to worry about finances.

Betty had then astonished him, by informing him that she was to inherit the entire business. They were very happy and planned to marry at the beginning of spring. Tim seemed to have recovered well and was a useful helper to the elderly landlord of the old Sheridan Inn.

***

It was with some dread that Florence Armitage handed her husband the letter with the official crest of the army on the envelope. She knew it would be the new placement for Stephen – he would have to go back. He could be sent anywhere.

She watched him open the letter and his eyes grow big. He held it out to her to read. He was to be placed at the Tavistock army camp as an Instructor! He would be able to get home regularly to see his heavily pregnant wife!

Florence celebrated this occasion by getting her dressmaker to make a number of outrageously flamboyant maternity dresses – made from the small-parlour curtains – which she wore with style.

Mother Benedicta had agreed with Florence's request for two good, well-trained girls from the Orphanage, to come to live with her and do the work of the huge house. The girls were splendid workers and greatly enjoyed working for this extraordinary lady who treated them like her own daughters.

***

One week after the death of Amelia, there was a Funeral service at the village Presbyterian Church. The building could not hold all the mourners.

For the second time in her life, Annie was sitting in the front pew, between Constable Potts and her son, Billy. Behind her sat Mrs Alice Norman, the minister's wife, Sam Watson and Penelope. Just about every person from the village was present, and a contingent of senior girls, all in uniform, was sent by special bus from the school, where Amelia had taught for so long.

The Reverend Herbert Norman preached on the very appropriate text: 'I have fought the good fight; I have run the course; I have kept the faith.' He was utterly unembarrassed by the tears that were trickling down his face as he preached – aware of the huge debt of gratitude he and his wife owed to the dead woman at the time of their own personal tragedy.

Both had loved her dearly.

At the end of the service the villagers formed a guard of honour all the way from the Church door to the cemetery in the Church grounds. As the coffin was carried out by Inspector Peters, Sergeant Pierce, Constable Watkins and Constable Manders, with one arm in a sling, they were followed by Potts walking with his arm around Annie, then Billy who walked with Mrs Alice Norman, then Sam and Penny.

As the cortege passed, Major Ted Waters, Major Tim Johnson and Captain Armitage – all in their dress uniforms – stood to rigid attention and saluted stiffly. The voices of the Church choir mingled with the tears and grief of the entire community, as the beloved and treasured, Amelia Hephzibah Tatley was lowered into the ground.

After the funeral, the solicitor visited Mr Norman, and informed him, that, apart from a gift of one hundred and fifty pounds to her dear young friend, Billy Watson – to further his education – the whole of Amelia's estate, her house and savings, were left to the minister for the relief of those suffering in any way.

The Will stated that such was the veneration in which Mr Norman was held by the whole village and by her own knowledge of him for nearly thirty years, Miss Tatley had every confidence that he would use the money to aid as many people as he could.

By the time the trial scheduled for Lady Emily Gascoigne-Ridley had arrived, it was determined that she was unfit to plead and was thus formally declared insane. She was then removed to the Asylum for the Criminally Insane, where she died, intestate, shortly afterwards.

Because of this, her immense fortune was forfeited to the crown – in reality, it became then part of consolidated revenue.

"Mr Bickerton and I have done our best," Dr Ernest Gascoigne-Ridley told Annie. "We've tried to get some of that huge fortune back to her only child, Monica. That poor woman has three children and another on the way and is very hard up.

"We've managed something at any rate. They've agreed to give us one of the houses – the big one at Vaucluse, or the other one, also large, at Double Bay. Whichever one we get will certainly be better than the tiny house where they are now. I know it's not much, out of that tremendous fortune, but it's something, at any rate."

***

Towards the end of the month, Hannah answered the door and saw with horror that the telegram-boy was standing, chewing gum nonchalantly, with his bike propped against the front door post. She took the telegram with shaking fingers, not uttering a word, and hurried back to the kitchen, afraid to open it.

She sat staring at the small envelope, then got to her feet and called loudly and urgently for Dan. He came running from the sheds but, seeing the telegram, turned as white as his mother. He made his mother sit down again, took the envelope and carefully and very slowly, with trembling fingers, opened it.

He flinched, and his mother cried: "One's dead isn't he? Which one, Dan? Oh, dear God, I cannot bear it."

"No ... it's Patrick, Mum," Dan's voice was choking on the words. "He's not dead. *He's been taken prisoner by the Japanese.*" Hannah gave a scream and took her head in her hands. Dan took her in his arms and his tears mingled with his mother's.

After a few minutes, Hannah sat up. "Dan, we've got to pray now as we've never prayed before. Every night now, after work, we'll say all our prayers together. It all depends on God now; nothing more can be done. Dear God ... the *Japanese*!

"The newspapers say terrible things about those little yellow people! Our only hope now is prayer. I'll get in touch with Annie right away. Will you join me, son?"

"Of course, I will Mum," Dan replied. "And I'll get Bianca to come up each night to join us too; she thinks of Patrick and Sean as part of her family as well." Before going back to work, Dan put on the kettle and made his mother drink a cup of strong tea, putting several spoons of sugar in her cup.

Walking back down the yard, there was an empty feeling inside of him; it didn't seem possible that one of the twins was a prisoner – actually a prisoner of the *Japanese*! It didn't seem possible ... They had never before even been away from home ... they had always been there ... they were only kids ...

Dan went behind the milking shed, and cried bitterly, hoping that those bloody useless girlie-farmers wouldn't see him. He resolved to see Bianca as soon as possible – *she* would understand and share his grief.

***

Telephone call from Mother Benedicta to her niece Annie Watson
When the telephone rang in the Watson house. Penelope answered it.

"Oh, Aunt Benedicta what a lovely surprise! Yes, I'm very well thank you …That's right, George and I are to be married in the spring; I'm hoping to bring him to see you as soon as he's free … What am I wearing?

"Well, Aunt, my mother suggested that we make a wedding dress out of some old, used white sheets, as we have no coupons for dress material …Yes, that does sound like her, doesn't it?" Penny laughed. "No, the truth is, we're hoping to be able to get a couple of faulty parachutes, as they're made of silk. Major Waters and Captain Armitage are on the lookout for a couple of them.

"What's that? No, I don't know how they know if they're faulty or not … Oh, wait a minute, please Aunt, my mother says she knows how they know. Yes, she's here, Aunt, bye." Annie took the phone.

"The way they test parachutes, Mother Benedicta," Annie spoke coldly, "is that they send up nosy, interfering members of the leisured classes, especially nuns, in an aeroplane and throw them out at twenty thousand feet. If the parachute doesn't open, then the person hurtles to the ground so no person of any importance is missed …

"Well, Aunt, it's true; I *am* angry with you; you might remember I nearly died as well as shooting a policeman – trying to do what you asked of me. If it hadn't been for the magnanimous kindness of Inspector Peters, I'd be wearing one of those repulsive prison gowns at the moment, for the term of my natural life.

"Anyhow, I've made up my mind, never, ever, ever again, no matter what, or who asks me, I'm not getting involved in trying to solve mysteries again. What's that? You have a problem? No, I beg of you, *don't* tell me! I don't want to know. I just *told* you I will not even consider it … Someone could die? What a load of rubbish…

"Nonsense, you're just being melodramatic. There's probably an easy solution … No, of course I've not the slightest intention of being involved in your problem but … What's that? Oh, he did, did he? Well, tell Inspector Peters to mind his own business … No! I've told you again and again …

"Well, of course, that's true – it *does* sound intriguing … Honestly, I have to admit it does interest me – not that I'm going to be involved in any way remember – but …just for academic interest… I would like to hear all the details …"

Sam Watson sitting near the fire with his daughter Penny, were listening to Annie on the phone. They both raised their eyebrows, pulled a face at each other and then they began to laugh helplessly.

***

While at that very moment in the pub, Bert Liveridge confided to his neighbour, Alf Cookson: "It's all part of the class struggle, you see, Alf. When the dawn of the Revolution occurs, it will be different …"

Bert stared into the middle distance, his mind visualising the fortune he almost had. Then the image of the dead Tanya flashed through his mind. He shuddered, quickly turning to his old friend.

"But never mind all that, Alf, get me another beer will you? You *won't*! Why, you lousy bugger! If I had taken the ten thousand pounds, I would've bought you a beer – in fact, I would've bought the whole pub. All right, all right, *all right*, I'll get it – I know it's my shout.

"What are you having?"